CHORISTERS' CAKE

"I know that you are trying to find out what sort of a person you are, and what kinds of things you can do; but, strange though it seems, the best way of becoming a real person, a real Peter Sandwell different from everybody else, is to forget yourself . . ."

Peter has other ideas. To assert his individuality, he deliberately rebels against school rules and customs. As a result he is sent to coventry by the other boys, who make it clear that unless he learns to pull his weight and accept his share of responsibilities, he will be ignored by all of them for the rest of the term.

But Peter remains defiant . . .

CHORISTERS' CAKE

is the second of William Mayne's
Choir School stories.
The first, also available
in Jade Paperbacks, is

A SWARM IN MAY

CHORISTERS' CAKE

WILLIAM MAYNE

Illustrated by
C. Walter Hodges

Jade Publishers
Haslemere

Jade Publishers
15 Stoatley Rise
Haslemere
Surrey GU27 1AF

First published 1956
First published in Jade Paperbacks 1990

Cover illustration by Tim Beer
Cover design by Samantha Edwards

Computer typeset by 'Keyword', Tring, Herts
Printed and bound by Cox & Wyman, Reading, Berks

British Library Cataloguing in Publication Data
Mayne, William *1928–*
Choristers' cake.
I. Title II. Hodges, C. Walter (Cyril Walter) *1909–*
823.914 [J]

ISBN 0–903461–41–2

CONTENTS

To Margaret Babington

CHAPTER 1

Rain Round the Cloisters

"Sometime Dean of this Cathedral Church", said the two lines of carved letters just below Peter Sandwell's eyes and between the next boy's feet. Whoever had put them there had not thought that one day the Cathedral choirboys would be standing on it during their PE lesson. Standing was not the right word: Peter Sandwell had both heels on it, and so had Meedman, just in front, but their knees were wide apart and their heads were between their knees: they were waiting for the football to be rolled along through the arches of legs, so that it could be raced round to the front of the team again.

Meedman felt Sandwell's head butt against his seat, so he sat as much as anyone can sit who looks for the time being like the two legs of a wishbone. Sandwell resisted the weight, but his head was pushed lower and lower. "Sometime Dean of this Cathedral Church" slid out of sight. He found he was looking down the rest of the sometime Dean's inscription, reading a Latin verse from above.

The football came down the tunnel, being paddled along from above by hand, slapping along the stone floor over the inscriptions, bringing with it a shadow that was not round, but pointed like an arch and graded from dark to light grey, with the different depths of the grey moving among themselves as the ball ran through the alternate shadow and light from the openings of the cloisters. It rolled along a little tunnel (of boys) inside a larger one (the north walk of the cloisters). Meedman guided the ball along his yard of tunnel, and passed it to Sandwell, who hit it a two-fisted biff when it rested for a moment on a cherub's tombstone face, and sent it flying down the cloister alone.

"Perfect idiot," said Trevithic, loudly, from the head of the team.

"Don't tell him," said Lowell, who had come up from the back of the other team and was now leading it.

"He's an augmented idiot," said Madington,

brushing his hair more on to the top of his head in case Trevithic barged into him bonily again.

"Sandwell," said Trevithic, "fetch it."

"Run, Sandy," said Meedman, removing his weight from Sandwell's shoulders.

"Me?" said Sandy, sitting down on the Latin verse and exchanging his view of the sometime Dean for one of bright coats of arms in the cloister vaulting.

The whole team lifted their heads and turned their bodies without moving their feet, and urged him to hurry. Sandy thought they looked like a row of startled looper caterpillars. The ball lay quietly against the door to the Bishop's garden. Sandy fetched it and ran forward to the head of the team with it. They bent themselves down as he ran past them. "Like the backbone skeleton of an animal," he thought, and fed the ball to Trevithic.

The other team finished four places ahead with a great shout that rolled round the cloisters and came out behind them again, but whether it went round a second time no one could tell, because they started the team game again.

"Do it properly this time, Sand*well*," said Mr Lewis. "Silly little *boy*. Don't send it round the *cloisters*. What will you think of *next*?" Mr Lewis's way of talking was the opposite of Dr Sunderland's, the organist. Dr Sunderland always faded into a rumbling grunt at the end of his sentences and words. Mr Lewis snapped his last word out loud and sharp. "Sforzando," said Trevithic, which is an instruction found in music, meaning "suddenly loud", and generally written *sfz* over the place where the loudness has to be. Everybody knew that Trevithic thought of Mr Lewis as having *sfz* written on the air above his head.

"It'll go too *far*. You'll find yourself dribbling it down the *nave*," said Mr Lewis, and "*Silly* little boy", for a change.

"Yes, sir," said Sandy.

"You'd better *not*," said Mr Lewis.

"No, sir," said Sandy. That was the right answer, but the others seemed to think he meant to say that he wanted to dribble the ball down the nave. Sandy had rather been thinking that it was not proper for Mr Lewis to call a senior a little boy, as if he thought seniority depended on other things than age. It depended on other things in choir, of course, but choir was nothing to do with Mr Lewis's PE lesson.

Sandy stood again over the sometime Dean and waited for the ball, raced it up to the front of the team, and hurled it back through Trevithic. The team finished first this time, and shouted before Stanhope, third man from last of the other side, had got to the front. Sandy looked at his big, disappointed eyes, and felt that victory was cruel when it dismayed people so good as Stanhope.

"Cheer up, *Stanners*," said Mr Lewis. "Each side has won a *game*. We'll go *in*, because it's eleven o'*clock*. You will not dash out into the rain as soon as we get to the other end of the Dark *Entry*."

"Exit, sir," said Trevithic.

"You will go in *twos*," said Mr Lewis. "I don't want a damp unhappy *scrum* in the school *doorway*. Right. At atten-*shun*. Don't gape, Kelsey. What is the subject of your *meditations*, Madington?"

"I was thinking, sir, that if they put glass all round the cloisters they could fill the middle with water and keep fish in it," said Madington. "An aquarium."

"Swimming pool, sir," said Trevithic. "High dives from the towers."

"It won't take long to fill," said Madington. "Not if it goes on raining like this."

"Stupid boy," said Mr Lewis. "Sandwell would put his fist through it and flood the *precincts*. Silence in the *ranks*." He looked up and down to see that the ranks were tidy, and came round alongside. "Right turn, right dress," he said.

Sandy waited for the order to left turn and march off round the corner and along the Dark Entry, along the gloomy passages under the Cathedral's out-buildings: the Chapter House, and the library, the new vestry and the stairs to the north-east transept. He was so busy preparing to be ready for the order, that when it came, to right turn and by the left quick march, he did not properly hear it, and turned left straight into Meedman: Mr Lewis had decided to march them all round the cloisters the long way. By the time Sandy had got out of the way and turned round, Meedman had become the file leader, alongside Paterson at the head of the other file. There was no place for Sandy to take. Mr Lewis had seen nothing of the mistake: he was looking across the cloisters to make sure there was nobody to get in the way of. Sandy ran forward between the files and marched in his proper place ahead of Meedman, without a partner.

It was not his fault that Meedman and Paterson at once shortened their steps, so that he drew farther and farther ahead of the rest. But Mr Lewis blamed him in a sforzando shout, and left him standing by the Bishop's garden door in a cold draught, while the rest wheeled left, and left twice more, brought themselves to the arch of the Dark Entry, and vanished into more and more quietness. Sandy stood at attention alone with the rain: no one else was in the cloister.

A spider ran quickly and silently among the tidewrack of the autumn's leaves. How did a spider stand to attention? How many legs did it use? Somebody came, not so quietly as the spider, along the Dark Entry. There were two people: Meedman and Paterson. Without a word they ranged themselves beside Sandy.

"What are you here for?" said Sandy, but they gave no answer. They stood for five minutes in silence, until Mr Lewis came to them. He surveyed all three for a minute.

"Mad children," he said at last. "Go *away*," and went away himself.

"Gone to buy food," said Meedman.

"What did you come back for?" said Sandy.

"We saved you, me and Pat," said Meedman. "We confessed our manifold sins and said it was our fault you got in front of us."

"It was my own fault, really," said Sandy.

"Was it?" said Paterson. "Then we needn't have confessed."

"Never mind," said Meedman. "Let's get wet: we've got to change anyway."

The way to get wet was to follow-my-leader Meedman in and out of the cloister arches: out into the showering rain, and back again round the mullions, all the way round to the Dark Entry. They left on the dry broad sill of the arcade a triple trail of wet plimsoll prints.

They met Dr Sunderland in the dark. He was moving his slow way along to his house at the other side of the Cathedral. He had farther to walk going this way round, but he would need to climb no steps except the three out of the cloisters.

"Mph," he said, meaning, "We meet again."

"Yes, sir," said Paterson.

"Been stretching 'mph lungs?" asked Dr Sunderland.

"All round the cloisters, sir," said Meedman. "If you

stretched lungs out flat, sir, they would cover a tennis court, sir."

"Can't play tennis now-a-daymph," said Dr Sunderland. "Not even on lungs, Meedmanph."

"No, sir," said Meedman.

"Some of you could do to stretch 'mph lungs," said Dr Sunderland. "You, Sandwe'mph, I mean. Could do with more exertion in next 'mfew weeks. Give you'mph opportunity if I canph."

"Yes, sir," said Sandy, not sure what Dr Sunderland meant.

Paterson knew, though, and as soon as Dr Sunderland had gone on he said, "It's the appointment of choristers, I think."

"Doesn't interest me," said Sandy.

"Well, you still aren't a chorister," said Meedman.

Sandy changed the subject. "Do you know, I think Dr Sunderland is going away from us as quickly as we are going away from him."

"If we run, will he get out of breath?" said Paterson, who didn't want to talk about chorister-making either.

"Let's choke him by whizzing back to school," said Sandy. "That'll chiz the chorister thing too."

CHAPTER 2

A Change in the Vestry

The three of them ran through the rain – getting no wetter than they already were, slapped another triple row of wet plimsoll prints on the old, red, rough tiles of the passage, and changed in the changing room, leaving bare, misty footprints on the new, smooth tiles. When they had dressed they went together to rescue the mid-morning cocoa. Madington was about to declare the list closed: he had already checked all the names but theirs, and Trevithic wanted to auction the remaining cocoa to anyone who would have it – Kelsey, for instance, who spent most of break attending the cocoa pot in search of dregs – and junior singing boys like Iddingley and Crew, who stayed partly for the cocoa and partly in the hope that Trevithic would kindly speak to them: if he did, they felt like newly-made barons for the rest of the day.

"You didn't expect us to bring it to the cloisters, did you?" said Trevithic.

"We didn't expect to *be* in the cloisters," said Sandy. "Stir it up more than that, Trevithic: I like the gritty stuff."

"Mud," said Madington. He waited until he saw them sip at their beakers before he ticked their names on the list.

"Take the things down to the kitchen," said Trevithic, and left them. Kelsey volunteered to take the cocoa pot, so that he could chew his way through the gravelly sugarless dregs. Before he had reached the dining-room door Stanhope stopped him, though Kelsey was more senior, and looked to see that Sandy, Meedman and Paterson had had their share, and went away again before he could be thanked.

"Well done, he," said Meedman, using the Choir School words of approval.

"Better than Kelsey," said Sandy. "Better than all the choristers."

"Except Trevithic," said Paterson.

"Trevithic only wants to be a doctor of music," said Sandy.

"So do I," said Paterson, dribbling his cocoa in his desire to say that he shared his ambitions with Trevithic.

"You're too absolutely musical," said Meedman. "At least, you aren't. And you've got a cocoa beard. Trevithic's absolutely musical, but Stanhope is going to be Prime Minister one day."

"So that he can put everything right," said Sandy. "And he says nobody will be senior to anybody."

"They'd be bound to be junior to *somebody*," said Paterson.

"We would be," said Meedman. "Same as we are now."

They took up the beakers, loaded them on to the tray, and took the tray to the kitchen, where they were scolded for being late. "You've got to have somebody to blame," said Meedman, when they had said that their lateness was the fault of Mr Lewis. "And it's best to blame seniors: if you blame juniors, that's a sort of bullying."

"Stanhope won't have any chizzes in the kingdom," said Sandy.

At the end of break there was a general announcement by Mr Ardent, the headmaster. He had to make the announcement separately to each class, interrupting the lesson to do so. Sandy's form, the fourth, were glad of the interruption. Mr Sutton, who was busy with irregular Latin verbs, was not, but he put down the chalk in the middle of "*ii, isti, iit*" and listened to Mr Ardent.

"At twelve o'clock we shall move cassocks and surplices from the crypt to the new vestry," said Mr Ardent. "At the same time, apparently, there will be a grand re-measuring of cassocks. The operation will take longer than I thought, Mr Sutton: the sewing people have only this moment told me they will be there."

"I am growing accustomed to the desecration of routine," said Mr Sutton. "But I fear that the classical graces" (he meant Latin) "are not easily acquired by the student who intermits for vestiary interests the pursuit of those graces."

"Perhaps if we regard the three sewing-ladies as the three Fates, we may be able to drag in some classical instruction," said Mr Ardent.

"Possibly," said Mr Sutton.

"They'll sew you up if you come unthreaded, sir," said Sandy. Mr Sutton merely picked up the chalk, and wrote "*iimus*" on the board.

Mr Ardent was about to go when Stanhope put up

his hand. "I knew my mother was coming to the Cathedral today, sir, but I didn't know it was for our cassocks. She didn't give me any message." His mother was one of the people who made and mended the Cathedral vestments and needlework stuffs like altar frontals and the velvet linings of the collection plates, and even the cloths used in the Treasury for washing and drying the gold and silver vessels of the Cathedral.

"Nobody knew until ten minutes ago," said Mr Ardent. "I think the weather has brought the Cathedral workmen indoors, and they want to take the old vestry down, now that the new one's ready." When he had gone, Mr Sutton went on with the lesson.

"I shall endeavour to lead you through the verb '*Eo*'," he said.

"Like the Christmas carol, sir?" said Paterson. "'Eo, eo, eo, let steeple bells be swungen'?"

"No," said Mr Sutton. "Do not attempt to unthread me, Paterson. The words 'thread' and 'fates' have an unfortunate connexion, which I think it worthwhile to acquaint you with – drawing good out of evil, as Mr Ardent suggested."

Mr Sutton's ten minutes of mythology helped the lesson a great deal, and the verb "*Eo*" was learnt quickly by almost everybody.

Mr Sutton was usually known as Brass Buttons, because his initials, C.U.S., looked something like the chemical symbols for copper and tin, particularly if you put the "n" of Sutton straight after the "S". Copper and tin make brass; Sutton makes button: and here he was, ready to become unthreaded at stupid people who were impolite or did not understand the difference between a gerund and a gerundive.

By being careful the fourth form kept him on his thread. There was one moment of danger when Meedman imagined into existence a word with three i's close together, which was bad enough; but when he tried to say it aloud, Mr Sutton glared and tapped the blackboard, where the word Meedman wanted was written, and allowed him to save himself.

At twelve o'clock Trevithic lined everybody up in the passage in strict order of choir seniority. Stanhope's mild remarks that alphabetical order was fairer than seniority had no effect: Stanhope would have been astonished if they had. Madington said that seniority was evolution like woodlice changing over the years into armadillos. Trevithic stopped the argument by marching them all out through the rain and into the Dark Entry. He unlocked the crypt door with his own key, and led them through the warm darkness to the back of the crypt. He had no need of the key to the vestry itself: the workmen had done away with the door by taking down the whole wooden wall that enclosed the cupboards.

"They've peeled the vestry," said Sandy.

"Don't start talking, Sandwell, " said Trevithic.

"No," said Mr Ardent. "Behave yourself, my boy. Remember where you are and why you're here at all." He had been in the vestry counting the ruffs in the ruff box. "Put on your cassocks, carry your jackets and your surplices, and line up again. There seems to be a lot of schoolboy treasure in some of these cupboards: will you take out what is yours and stow it tidily in your jackets, so that it won't be seen as you walk through the Cathedral – and don't put it in the new vestry: take it back to school. Choristers first: go on, Trevithic."

The long tail was made up of the whole choir: the whole school, in fact, all but the newest boys, who did not yet wear cassocks. They went one by one into the dark vestry: the workmen had undone the electric wires, so there was no light. Sandy thought the line of boys was like a new bicycle chain being run for the first time into a dark black pit of oil – going in blue-grey, like steel, and coming out purple (some strange modern oil, perhaps) with the white surplices bright like polished steel hung across their arms.

Sandy had only one thing in the vestry, but he particularly hoped it would not be seen: a long rope of forty-eight conkers, strung on one of Lowell's old 'cello strings. Conkers were being kept out of sight at present: Madington had heard Mr Ardent complain about conker fragments all over the school – "Twelve basketfuls," said Madington – so Trevithic, although he had a champion 186-er, had ordered all conkers out of sight for a fortnight. Sandy used to take a handful into service each day and train them into fighting trim by kneading them in his fingers one at a time, and polishing them on the hem of his cassock, working wax from the stump of an altar candle into the hole with a matchstick, to make the conker heavy and solid. People used to use chewing gum, but that substance had been forbidden in a very strong way by Mr Ardent.

The long coil of conkers, wound round itself three times, could be hidden in an empty jacket sleeve, and was safely there by the time Sandy left the vestry. When everybody had passed through, and the last probationers (who wore no surplices) sorted out, Trevithic led them off again, while Mr Ardent turned the switches so that the vestry lights upstairs would work.

The choir filed across the crypt among the pillars and chairs, and twisted its way up to the Treasury, where it arranged itself in full choir order in front of the gilded clock with the pendulum that must not be touched, but could so easily be. Decani stood on the right, Cantoris on the left. They walked solemnly along the north choir aisle, through the north-east transept, along a passage above the Dark Entry, and into a room that would have looked out over the cloisters if there had been a window to it.

The sewing people were there already and, as soon as Mr Ardent came, everyone was checked and measured to see that his cassock fitted and that his surplices were the right length. Sandy edged himself out of order so that Mrs Stanhope would be the one to look over his cassock for gaping seams and dropped hems or loose ruff buttons. He hoped she would ask him whether he was a friend of Michael's. She said nothing but "Dear, dear", when she saw the worn conker-polishing patch on the inside of the cassock hem.

When they were dismissed, in twos and threes, Sandy had to hang the conkers behind his best surplice in the locker he shared with Meedman. He was released at the same time as Stanhope, and he wanted to say "I like your mother, Michael", but the thought of using a Christian name at school was too much for him, so he said nothing, and they went back to Mr Lewis's history lesson in silence. Sandy could find nothing to say to anyone so admirable as Stanhope.

"Cheer up, *Stanners*," said Mr Lewis. "No good starting miserable when we're learning about the death of Mary, Queen of *Scots*."

CHAPTER 3

The Cake Offered

Towards the end of Mr Lewis's history lesson, which went from Mary, Queen of Scots, to the sighting of the Spanish invasion fleet off the Lizard, Sandy had let his mind leave the subject and float off into a complicated witty conversation (meant to make him famous) about Armadas and armadillos, and Madington's theory of woodlice turning into armadillos, and the really witty, but hard to arrange, part of the conversation concerned Drake playing bowls: a game played with balls called woods. The joke went somehow woodlice, woods, armadillos, Armada. The only question was, did it make sense, or nonsense of Madington's idea? For the best results it should make nonsense of Madington and uphold Stanhope.

There was a silence in Sandy's thoughts and a silence in the room. Mr Lewis was looking at him.

"They were attacked by *what*, Sandwell?"

Sandy used the witty conversation all up together in one sentence: "The woods by woodlice, and the Armada by armadillos, sir."

"Is this a *joke*?" said Mr Lewis.

"Yes, sir," said Sandy. "Or a sort of idea."

"Write out an explanation, and bring it to me by *bedtime*," said Mr Lewis. He stopped talking about history and started to give them notes to copy instead.

"Idiot," said Meedman. "Messing up a lesson."

"I hope you mean Sandwell, not *me*," said Mr Lewis. "If you won't *listen*, you'll have to *write*. 1587, Mary, Queen of *Scots*, executed at *Fotheringay* . . ."

Only Stanhope did not mind writing. His notes went down, word after word neat as stitching and always ready before anyone else.

The bell rang in Calais Roads, with fireships sailing down among the enemy.

"A few more words, sir," said Paterson.

"No," said Mr Lewis, and went off to wash the chalk dust from his face before dinner.

"*Nothing* but notes in this place," said Meedman, feeling, like everybody else, disagreeable when he was hungry. "If it isn't musical notes it's historical ones. Sandy's fault."

"I only said it to disagree with Madington," said Sandy: disagreeing with Madington meant agreeing with Stanhope, but Stanhope seemed to notice nothing in the remark, and went to wash his hands, though any other owner would have called them clean already.

After dinner there was a rest for the whole school: boarders on their beds, and day-boys who had stayed to dinner sitting in the classrooms. Even Mr Lewis was in a chair sleeping: Trevithic woke him in a different way each day. This afternoon he borrowed Lowell's little tenon saw and a piece of wood, and knelt behind Mr Lewis's chair pretending to saw through the chair leg. Mr Lewis woke with such energy that Trevithic spent five minutes gargling out of his throat the sawdust he had been made to swallow. What was left on the carpet Madington put into Mr Lewis's tobacco jar.

There was a full practice on Wednesdays: that is, men as well as boys. Dr Sunderland greeted them when he came last to the practice room, with "Mph, jumph", missing out his words entirely and leaving in the grunt only, and meaning good afternoon, gentlemen.

The practice room was high up in the Cathedral at the top of a steep narrow staircase, and Dr Sunderland, very punctual for full practices, had had to hurry his heaviness up sideways.

Mr Ardent was among the lay clerks today. There was a great lack of men to sing, so Mr Ardent sang from his Minor Canon's stall when he took the daily services. When he was part of the choir he sang a high part, alto, and when he was a priest he sang tenor, so he had to change voices between each versicle and response, and

25

between each prayer and its amen. When Mr Ardent was not in the Cathedral, Trevithic had to leave the Decani treble and sing alto instead. Lowell, next to him, hated an alto as a neighbour, so if you saw him turn his back on Trevithic and face Canon Fredley at the west end of the choir, you knew that Trevithic was singing alto.

"Mph?" said Dr Sunderland again as he sat at the piano. It was a question to Trevithic, meaning: "Has everybody a copy?" Trevithic nodded. "Te Deumph," said Dr Sunderland, naming next Sunday's morning music. He went through the things that might be difficult in the music. There was so much different music that the choir only sang through it two or three times a year: hardly anything was known by heart. "You aren't here to learn'mph," Dr Sunderland would say. "Sing'mph and forget'mph. Some of 'mph's good, some of 'mph's bad, and 'mph rest's horrid." He would hardly ever say which was good, bad or horrid, but he had told Trevithic once that he too often preferred the horrid. Today he warned the basses about a tricky lead on page eight, telling them where to remember their note from, and warned Cantoris trebles about a soft passage and the way it grew louder.

Dubnet moved from his place to close the door firmly and keep the sound in the room. Dr Sunderland began to play, and the choir sang to itself the week's music, and looked at what was to come.

At five past three the lay clerks went – all the men but Mr Ardent, who stayed behind as if he had something to say. He had. He spoke first quietly with Dr Sunderland, who was writing Sunderlandish ideas about accompani- ments on the edge of the organ music.

"Carry onph," said Dr Sunderland. "Not you, Dubnet, Owenph. Mr Ardent 'mphing to say."

"Item one," said Mr Ardent. "Some people are still leaving things in vestry lockers. If they are not removed, Kelsey, Dubnet, Crew and, of course, Sandwell, immediately after evensong, they will vanish for ever. There is plenty of room in school to store things. You have been warned. The other thing Dr Sunderland will tell you about. Choristers can go, I suppose, Dr Sunderland?"

"Better stay," said Dr Sunderland. "When's 'mph Dean going away, Mr Ardent?"

"The seventh of November," said Mr Ardent. "Less than three weeks' time."

"Some of you must stretch 'mph lungs," said Dr Sunderland. "Time I appointed another chorister'mph. Don't know whom'ph. Test for all senior singing boys Sat'day week. Some of you should have been choristers already," and he looked straight at Sandy, who knew it was true. "Pull up 'mph socks, do 'mph bit of work 'mphstead 'mph letting Trevithic do it all, Decani; or Madingtonph, Cantoris."

"The idea is that the Dean will be here to make you a chorister, if you pass the test," said Mr Ardent. "If he doesn't make you before he goes away, you'll have to wait until next term, as far as I can see; and by then Stanhope's cake will be harder than the shelf it's been standing on these last few months."

"Lowell could saw it up," said Trevithic.

"The Dean and Chapter have to eat it," said Mr Ardent.

"I'm sorry we've kept it so long, Michael," he said to

Stanhope, "we've been waiting for a partner to share it."

"Yes, sir," said Stanhope.

Sandy looked at Stanhope, who looked at him, then away. Sandy decided at once that Stanhope would not like to share the cake with him, though if it had been Sandy's own cake he would let Stanhope have it all if he wanted, and go without one himself. Besides, why try to be a chorister, which was only making a senior out of yourself, when Stanhope's idea was that there should be no seniors or juniors, only alphabetical order: perhaps that would bring him and Stanhope very close together.

The cake itself was what each chorister had to provide for the Dean and Chapter and the rest of the choristers and singing boys. In the old days it was two bottles of wine, as a way of saying thank you for being made a chorister and earning ten pounds a year. Nowadays it was a cake and, after providing the Dean and each member of the Chapter and choir with a piece, the chorister ate the rest himself, gradually. To save the expense of the cakes and of the blue icing that decorated them, they were shared between two choristers, so sometimes a cake increased in age and hardness until another chorister was made. Dr Sunderland appointed the choristers, but the Dean made them, at a ceremony during evensong. At some time after that, when it was convenient, the chorister cut his cake and shared it round.

Dr Sunderland had one more thing to say. "Got idea one of you senior choristers should have 'mph badge. Hard work earns 'mph, not old age. Dean can do 'mph when he does chorister'mph. That all. Go."

Owen and Dubnet led the way down the narrow

stairs into the Treasury.

"Now," said Trevithic, not letting them go at once. "I don't see why all Decani shouldn't be choristers, and all the choristers badge boys."

"Nor me why Cantoris shouldn't," said Madington.

"You people," said Trevithic. "They sound like a Sunday School treat sitting in the rain at Bude."

"Always rains in Cornwall," said Madington.

Turle, a virger, came out from the inner Treasury, where his silver wand was kept. "Go on," he said. "Gossip in the vestry, not here. I heard somebody privily slandering his neighbour." That was almost a quotation from the day's psalms: Turle's favourite habit. They had just sung the Psalms upstairs, and they would sing them again in a few minutes' time.

"Who also hath a proud look," said Trevithic: he was as good as Turle at Psalm-quoting. Turle scowled: he knew that the rest of the verse was about a "high stomach"; and that Trevithic was referring to his fatness. "Go on," said Turle. "You'd better hurry up."

Trevithic led them to the vestry. "Before you go out of here after service I want to talk to Decani," he said.

"They need it," said Madington. "Cantoris will be very polite to their poor relations and keep out of the way."

CHAPTER 4

Trevithic Draws Cover

After service Trevithic kept all Decani in again, to tell them of something he intended to do. "Not choristers," he said. "Unless they want to."

"What is it?" said Lowell, who was surprised that Trevithic should have anything new to say to Decani without telling him first.

"Extra practice for singing boys," said Trevithic. "In the practice room at break each day. Dr Sunderland might make two choristers if they're very good."

"We shan't want the little titches," said Lowell.

"They might as well all come," said Trevithic. "They'll be choristers all the sooner if they do some extra now. And if the choristers come, one of them might be badge boy in the end."

"Dr Sunderland won't take an extra practice," said Lowell. "Not of only half the choir, either."

"I'll take the practice, of course," said Trevithic. "I'm going to ask Dr Sunderland now, in case Madington gets there first."

"We'll all go," said Silverman. His ideas were generally useless and unworkable – all right only if you had a disciplined army and plenty of time and were doing something that depended on noise and strength.

This idea was a good one, though.

"Come on," said Trevithic. "Line up in two lines: we'll catch him before he escapes from the organ loft."

They went back into the Cathedral. Trevithic tidied every tie and made them pull out jacket flaps and straighten socks. "Why do you wear a dishcloth instead of a shirt, Owen?"

Dr Sunderland had finished the Voluntary – the music after the service – and come down from the loft, hung the key in its secret place, and gone on his way home down the steps towards the nave. Trevithic, hearing the music stop and seeing the lamp over the console extinguished, split Decani into two groups, one to go down the choir aisle and the other to go down the choir, to trap Dr Sunderland whichever way he went.

They nearly missed him entirely. Trevithic, leading his detachment through the choir, met Turle, who said, "The Cathedral isn't a short cut, young man."

"We are looking for Dr Sunderland," said Trevithic, leading his column on.

"He's gone," said Turle, standing in the way. "You can go back and go round."

"It's urgent," said Trevithic, and went on, going suddenly round Turle and round the brass eagle of the lectern. Turle could only order without authority, and grumble without being able to express more than his own opinion of how a Cathedral (and its choir) ought to be run.

The other column had run into a knot of people on the steps under the tower, and to avoid being talked to by complete strangers who want to know elementary things they might have guessed, Lowell had to lead the

party into the north aisle of the nave and Dr
Sunderland was in the south aisle, beyond the thickets
of chairs full of prowling people. Dr Sunderland was
halfway to the door, and already unfurling his
umbrella. The flying squad hastened down the length
of the nave, and crossed it at the clear west end in
front of the great door. But when they reached the
clock-tower door, which Dr Sunderland should have
been aiming for, he had turned round and gone back
eastwards up the nave.

"Going out by the other door," said Lowell. "Must
be going to see Canon Fredley or somebody."

"Too many people in the place, as well as too many
pillars," said Silverman. "And you can't hurry or crawl
here." He would have liked to execute this organist-
catching manoeuvre in a forest.

"Lead on again," said Lowell. "And beware of
Turle in the choir, Tweedling about." Turle and
Dr Sunderland were nicknamed Tweedledee and
Tweedledum, because of their fatness.

They went back along the south side of the nave.
"Lost and gone for ever," said Lowell, when he found
that Dr Sunderland was not in the transept. "I don't
know where he is."

Trevithic had come out of the choir, not seen Dr
Sunderland and lost sight of Lowell's column, and led
his own party down the steps and into the north aisle of
the nave where Lowell had been before, thinking that
Lowell would certainly have gone the other way. So
each party went once round the nave, and met on the
steps under the tower after a little modest semaphore
between Lowell and Trevithic. Dr Sunderland was
nowhere to be seen.

"He didn't go out of the transept door," said Lowell. "He must have gone into the cloisters,"

"Follow him," said Trevithic.

Stanhope noticed a light in the organ loft on the choir screen, above the row of stone kings. Somebody moved about up there. Trevithic identified the click of the organ music cupboard being closed, and they all heard Dr Sunderland's feet on the top three wooden steps of the little staircase in the screen.

"Caught," said Trevithic. They went up the wide steps under the tower and into the doorway that led to the choir, and waited for Dr Sunderland to appear.

"Hello," said Lowell. "The enemy comes."

"He won't do anything," said Trevithic. "I've just beaten him off."

"Not Turle," said Lowell. "Madington."

Madington had come quietly down the choir and was waiting with them.

"What do you want?" said Trevithic.

"An invention of my own," said Madington. "What do you people all want?"

"An invention of *our* own," said Lowell. "Trevithic's going to give us all extra practices, but we thought we'd better ask Great Tom Tweedledum."

"I can ask him as well," said Madington. "For Cantoris. What time did you think of the idea, Trevithic?"

"Just after service," said Trevithic. "But I knew I was going to think of it just before, in the Treasury."

"I thought of it absolutely before we put on our surplices," said Madington. "That's why I took Cantoris over to school without waiting for you: I had to ask them whether they would do it."

33

"Would they?" said Trevithic.

"They all agreed," said Madington. "But I suppose you had to *order* your lot. Anyway, I thought of it first, so I ask first."

"All right," said Trevithic, who thought he was fairly beaten.

Silverman and Lowell, though, looked at each other and exchanged a word. They had to act quickly: Dr Sunderland was opening the door at the bottom of the staircase. Together, at a moment when Turle was not looking, Lowell and Silverman opened the door of the Dean's stall and tipped Madington into it among the red silk, and closed the door on him again.

"Beware Turle," said Stanhope. "And don't rip up that silk: the Dean's bad enough as it is."

"Well done, ye," said Trevithic. Madington lay quiet in the stall, crouched low so that Turle would not guess he was there.

Dr Sunderland appeared. "'Mph?" he said, frowning at everybody in the gloom of the archway.

"This is Decani, sir," said Trevithic. "We thought we'd like some extra practice during break each day."

"Can't help 'mph," said Dr Sunderland. "Too much else to do 'mph next week or so possibly able help 'mph."

"We don't need your *help*, sir," said Trevithic. "Only your permission to use the practice room."

"Practice 'mph yourself?" said Dr Sunderland. "Good idea, Trevithic. I don't mind. What about Cantoris, 'mph?"

"They decided not to ask you, sir," said Lowell.

"'Mph," said Dr Sunderland. "They don't need so much practice as you people: Trevithic does all 'mph

34

work for youmph. But if he sweats you now 'mph takes no nonsense from Sandwemph, I daresay somebodymph be choristermph."

"That's what we thought," said Trevithic, looking at Sandy.

"Is that so?" said Sandy to himself. "Very funny, Trevithic." But whatever they thought they hadn't forgotten him.

Dr Sunderland put away the key and went down the steps again. Turle came in his slow-looking quick walk down the choir. "Come on, you boys," he said. "Outside with you, in everybody's way, pestering Dr Sunderland. Be off with you."

"Goodbye," said Trevithic, and led Decani off down the steps and into the cloisters.

"Shall I go and rescue Madington?" said Stanhope. "You don't want him to be caught, do you?"

"I'll go with you," said Sandy; but Trevithic said "Only one go: Stanhope", so Stanhope went and brought Madington down safely.

"If I'd had a periscope I'd've been able to escape before," said Madington. "Anyway, thanks for putting me in there: I found out that we don't need so much practice as *some* people."

"Aren't you even going to have a revengeful fight?" said Trevithic, getting ready to run.

"Of course," said Madington. "No hair-pulling." He handed his spectacles to Lowell to look after, and chased Trevithic politely among the cloisters and through the Dark Entry. Chasing had to be done politely, so that it would not look rowdy. Lowell took the rest of Decani back in a proper orderly way, because they hadn't walked back from service yet. They

met Trevithic sweeping the school passage with
Madington's hair whilst Madington tried to strangle
Trevithic with his feet.

CHAPTER 5

He that hath Ears

The weather dried towards Wednesday evening, and just before darkness there was a squinting flash of sun from the golden windflags on the Cathedral tower. Paterson saw it from the kitchen window during washing up, as the flags swung in the wind.

"Sparks," he said. "When the wind blows they get brighter."

"I wonder what the Cathedral windows would be like if they were made of coloured sparks," said Sandy.

"Only seventeen days to the fifth of November," said Meedman. "I saw fireworks in the shops on Saturday."

"Too much talking," said Kelsey. "Those knives aren't dry."

"They're hot: they'll get dry," said Sandy. "You just leave us alone, Kelsey; we can manage."

"Somebody will about kill you one day," said Kelsey, but he was not allowed to try it himself in the kitchen. He went with a cloth to wash the tables down.

Mr Lewis arrested Sandy on the way to bed. "What have you been doing this *evening*?" he said.

"Playing Mah-Jong," said Sandy. "I got 'Moon in the bottom of the Sea' and chizzed everybody."

"What about my explanation of your joke during *history*?" said Mr Lewis.

"I forgot it, sir," said Sandy.

"I don't blame you," said Mr Lewis. "It wasn't a very good *joke*. You'd better spend tomorrow's *break* recopying your last two pages of *notes*, in case you wrote them down without *understanding*. Don't *forget*."

"No, sir," said Sandy, and went to bed pleased rather than sorry. Trevithic's practice during break would be one short, which seemed sensible if the one not there had no desire to become a chorister. Besides, the whole thing would chiz Trevithic: no one else dared to do such a thing. If he could score over Trevithic that would be something Stanhope could notice him for. Sandy went to bed thinking of a long sequence of conversation, starting with the putting-down of Trevithic and ending with Stanhope inviting Sandy himself to Downing Street and offering him half the kingdom – by permission of the Queen, of course. Trevithic could look on, rather old and rather fat, like Dr Sunderland and other doctors of music.

Thursday morning kept Wednesday's evening promise and was fine, though from upper windows clouds could be seen in the west, where the wind came from. The wind was warm and strong, and blew the fallen leaves from the trees and heaped them in corners and stirred them so that they looked like banks of living fire under the walls. Meedman, thinking not of the appearance of fire in the leaves now but of fire-to-be in sixteen days' time, wanted to gather them up and keep them dry.

"Nowhere to put them," said Sandy. "Only the prefects' hut. But it would chiz them too much: it wouldn't be safe." Not all the prefects were so patient as Trevithic and Madington: some of them would deal with things in their own rapid way with fists or a thick book on the back of the head – Boyce's *Cathedral Music* was one of the heaviest – and that kind of being dealt with, though it hardly defeated brainwork and witty chizzes, did make you think about something else for a time. Of course, a B.C.M. on the head was fair reward for an ordinary piece of cheek, but it could not stop you winning if the chiz was a fair one, like Sandy's idea of evading Trevithic's practice: not merely staying away, but having somebody else's orders to obey as well; the result should be that you won without getting into trouble.

The prefects' hut was one of the Dean's potting sheds, built against the back of the school. A long time ago the prefects had commandeered it, built it a chimney, and nailed the tiles firmly in place. They kept there two Cathedral chairs, any number of candle ends and a store cupboard full of cake. Over the fireplace hung a kettle, and on the back of the door a row of cups, and in the proper season of the year there was a bowl of flowers on the table. There was a little heap of bones, found in the precincts by Madington, and painted blue: he hoped one day to make a whole monk's skeleton from them.

No one was allowed in the hut but the prefects and the landlord, the Dean, but he had never come there. Even Mr Ardent asked permission before venturing inside.

Sandy, remembering Stanhope's theory of no seniority, thought that ideas were of little use without action, in the same way as action (being punched by a prefect) was of little use against ideas (the prefect didn't change the idea by punching you). Sandy put the idea into action by walking across the hall after breakfast, going round Trevithic who was reading the paper on the floor, and going out of the hall door and into the garden. He was allowed in none of these places, but Mr Ardent was in the kitchen trying to catch up on breakfast, which he had missed by taking an early service.

The garden was empty, and Sandy passed the four big windows without being called back, and went round behind the school. Here he was nearly caught by Madington, who was in the hut with another prefect: who it was Sandy could not see. Madington thought the coast was clear, put the hut door to and lit a candle.

"We'll get some more sackfuls when we get some more sacks," he said. "Last year we tipped it all on the floor and it was never tidied up and Mr Ardent wouldn't come to the Christmas Eve feast. I'll go with Trevithic later on: he can always get things from the workmen."

"Careful with the candle, then," said the other person – probably Beale, next senior to Madington – "it's very short."

"Only one thing to say," said Madington. "Trevithic will be here in a moment: he's only filling his mind with unsorted facts by reading the newspaper."

Sandy, behind a buttress, found that he could not turn back if Trevithic was about to come, nor could he, for the same reason, stay where he was. He had to go on. He tiptoed across the grass, and climbed up on the Dean's soft compost heap among the withering nettles, and crouched behind the hut with his ear against the roof, because the compost heap was halfway up the wall.

"We'll chiz Decani," said Madington. "We'll go up and practise during break, and not give them a chance at all. Then we're bound to have the new chorister in Cantoris."

"And the badge boy," said Beale – it *was* Beale: Sandy found a gap under the curled edge of a Roman tile and looked in. Beale and Madington were sitting by candle-light sorting out cake from the cupboard. They sat on two sacks stuffed with something, not on the chairs.

"I expect you'll be badge boy," said Madington.

"I'd better be, I suppose," said Beale, very pleased at Madington's thinking he might be.

"Don't want Silverman or somebody on Decani to have it," said Madington. "Anyway, if we tell all

Cantoris to rush to the practice room before Decani, we can slightly chiz them."

"They'll besiege us," said Beale.

"Only for twenty minutes," said Madington. "And it'll be a good victory and an absolute win."

"What will?" said Trevithic, opening the door. "Who came out just now? I'm sure somebody did, after you two."

"You did," said Madington. "Joke over."

"Wit," said Trevithic. "Isn't this cake awful?"

Sandy escaped quietly. The wind pitched in the roofs and in the Dean's trees, so that noises were swallowed in other noises or whirled away with the leaves. He hurried back to the hall, crossing it at a clear moment when only Mr Sutton was there, rummaging in his bookcase, still wearing his cycling cape. He was putting away his bicycle pump, for safety. He waited until Sandy had gone before hiding it finally.

Three minutes later Lowell rang the bell for practice. Sandy waited by the door to the hall for Trevithic. It seemed obvious that he could only chiz Trevithic if the practice were held; and by telling Trevithic of Madington's plot he could at once chiz Madington, and later chiz Trevithic. He was winning all the time, and working like a mole underground: everything depended on him.

He separated Trevithic from the others boldly, as an important messenger might, by pulling him back: it made another little victory, because it annoyed Trevithic and Trevithic could do nothing about it. It annoyed him so much that he did not bother to say thank you for Sandy's information, but at least he did not seem to think that any sneaking was involved. There was, Sandy supposed, rather a war between Decani and Cantoris.

Trevithic said nothing. He linked the whole choir up and marched them across to the Cathedral. The wind, leaping down into the cloisters and along the Dark Entry, held them back all the way, and shortened their stride so that they had eight more paces to make; but Madington was the only one to notice it, and he tied a knot in his handkerchief to remind him to see whether it took eight less walking back afterwards with the wind behind.

Mr Ardent was in the vestry pinning up the typed list of which locker was which, and who had what sized surplice and ruff, so that the right things were put in the right place when Mrs Stanhope or the two other sewing people changed them over for laundry.

"I think I gave you fair warning," said Mr Ardent. "I had to look in each locker to check the list, and all those things that were left there have gone. The rule stands for all time: nothing in these lockers but cassocks and surplices. You've only yourselves to thank."

"No, I haven't," thought Sandy, looking to find that his rope of conkers had indeed gone. "It's Trevithic's fault, but I'll rechiz him by not being at practice, and that'll make him all low."

CHAPTER 6

Secret Orders

Madington was surprised to find that walking back to school after service with the wind behind took as many paces as walking into the wind. But he worked out why, and announced the general result: "Into the wind the pressure holds your legs back, and with the wind behind you hold them back yourself to avoid being blown along too fast: you take as many steps either way."

"And you might be blown over if you're standing on one leg for long," said Lowell.

"Like a stork," said Madington.

"Cabbage stalk," said Sandy, but the others said only "Wit", and took no more notice.

In the five minutes before the next lesson Lowell went round to all Decani with a message from Trevithic. "Don't go to the practice room today," he said. "We've decided to let Cantoris have it today."

"Why?" said Sandy: this was defeat before the battle began.

"Trevithic said so."

"But he really wants a practice, doesn't he?" said Sandy.

"Of course," said Lowell. "But you know what you told him? Well, he doesn't want to be chizzed, so he isn't going to do anything about it. Elementary."

"Not so good," said Sandy. He went to tell Trevithic so, but thought it might be dangerous, and stopped Silverman instead, whom Lowell had just spoken to.

"It might have been a battle," said Sandy, knowing that the idea would appeal to Silverman.

"It's a pity," said Silverman. "How did Trevithic know about Madington?"

"I told him," said Sandy. "If I hadn't, there would have been a battle."

"Yes," said Silverman, regretting that there wasn't. "Was it true, Sandy?"

"Quite true," said Sandy. "But I wanted to have a practice for Decani."

"Tell everybody in Decani to go up as soon as the bell goes," said Silverman. "Simple: nobody would ever know that it wasn't Trevithic that said so, they'll only think he's changed his mind again."

"And we could tell Cantoris that Madington said don't go," said Sandy.

"I'll do that," said Silverman. "I can tell Kelsey, and he'll do it."

"Then I'll tell Decani," said Sandy. "It's really a way of bossing Trevithic about."

"Well done, we," said Silverman.

Sandy went to find and tell all the members of Decani – except, of course, Trevithic who was to find out the altered arrangement at break. He began with people like Owen and Iddingley, telling them to tell the rest. He was careful to say only, in case anything went wrong, that there would be a practice, not that Trevithic had ordered it.

"Changes his mind," said Iddingley. "Like a

45

weathercock."

This telling people to do things without having to say who said so seemed a useful way of doing things, particularly when Trevithic and Madington would find themselves doing what they had decided not to do. But Sandy would have thought again if he had known that Silverman forgot at once the whole conversation and went instead to disturb Dubnet and Crew racing model cars down the passage.

By the time the bell went for the next lesson the word had gone round Decani, and Sandy had been told twice by juniors what he had already told Owen and Iddingley. At the end of the lesson Mr Sutton was almost pushed from the fourth form room by Decani and Cantoris alike, all jostling to be ahead. From the door of the fourth form Sandy watched them walking in the passage so that school rules were not broken. Outside, though, they all ran. Sandy saw the last of them, wondered what would happen, and went back into the fourth form to start on the two pages of history notes.

Mr Ardent came from the kitchen, and, passing the noticeboard, studied it for a while, took down a notice, and carried it away with him. Sandy went to see what was taken. It was the prefects' list, the list of people who had offended against the school rules or cheeked the prefects, and who were dealt with every now and then by Mr Ardent and the prefects in committee. Sandy's name was on it for fooling about in the dormitory, but he hoped nothing much would happen.

While he was in the passage, he thought of going up to the dining-room for his cocoa, which he and everybody else had forgotten about. He found Trevithic there supervising the cocoa pot, and instead of Madington with the book there was a very small probationer who seemed almost frightened of the pencil he had to use, and just as frightened of Trevithic and the two other Decani prefects, although there were seven more probationers drinking cocoa.

"Where's everybody else, Sandwell?" said Trevithic.

"Gone to the practice room," said Sandy.

"What for?" said Trevithic. "Has Decani gone?"

"Yes," said Sandy. "And I think Cantoris must have gone as well."

"We let them," said Trevithic. "Why shouldn't they?"

"I told them not to," said Sandy, glad to show whose power was ordering everybody from place to place.

"They seem to have gone, all the same." said Trevithic. "I wonder what they're doing."

"No idea," said Sandy. "I'm doing something for Mr Lewis." He took his cocoa and began to drink it.

"Come on," said Trevithic. "You know what an idiot Sandwell is: he might have said *anything*." He and Lowell went, leaving DeMaris, the other prefect, to ladle out the cocoa into the beakers, which he did very badly, spilling it all over the tray.

The probationers looked at Sandy, as if, he thought, they were measuring up their ideas of what an idiot was like, after hearing what Trevithic had said.

Mr Ardent came along the passage again, carrying his mid-morning cup of tea. "There's nobody outside yet," he said, and "There's nobody inside either," when he saw the almost empty room. "Where are they all? Oh, my dear DeMaris, what a mess. Hold the ladle higher up."

"I am not used, sir, to ladling things," said DeMaris.

"I'll do it," said Mr Ardent. "Will you go and find Trevithic for me. I want to hold a prefects' meeting: there seems to be a long list of wicked sinners on the board."

"They're all in Cathedral, sir," said DeMaris. "Trevithic's gone to bring them back, sir, before they do anything wrong."

"Wrong?" said Mr Ardent. "Why have they gone into the Cathedral at all?"

"It was Trevithic's idea, sir, to take an extra practice for Decani, but Cantoris are trying to use the room at the same time, and Trevithic has run across, sir, with Lowell, to stop them all."

"Most confusing," said Mr Ardent. "Trevithic can manage them, but I wonder if I ought to go across in case they have done anything foolish. What will they be up to next?"

DeMaris abandoned the ladle, leaving Mr Ardent to it.

The probationers finished their cocoa quietly and went, looking as if they sensed something wrong. Sandy, too, felt that the atmosphere was rather alive with judgement, and he realized that he was the only singing boy or chorister in the building. The probationer with the cocoa-book and the pencil finished his cocoa and started on the pencil. Sandy drank down the silt in the bottom of the beaker and put the beaker on the tray.

"Don't go outside, Sandwell," said Mr Ardent. "We shall want you soon."

"No, sir," said Sandy, not mentioning that he would not go out in any case because of Mr Lewis's history: things like that were best not talked about to Mr

Ardent.

Halfway through the word "recusancy", towards the beginning of Elizabeth's reign, the rest came back under Trevithic's leadership. Madington was head of the column walking with bowed head: Trevithic, though leader, walked beside the column. Madington blew his nose by the fourth-form door, and Sandy saw that behind his spectacles there were tears.

"Go up and get your cocoa," said Trevithic. "And you can all stay in the dining-room while I see Mr Ardent."

Stanhope broke from line and came across to Madington.

"Back into line, Stanhope," said Trevithic, but Stanhope took no notice until he had brought from his pocket a clean folded handkerchief and given it to Madington, who immediately put it to his eyes. Stanhope's handkerchiefs were the best in the school, as fine as feathers, with his name in open embroidery on the hem. He went back into the line among the singing boys, and walked with them to the dining-room.

Madington dealt with all his outlying tears, polished his spectacles, sniffed, mopped for tears again, blew his nose, and followed Trevithic to the dining-room.

Instead of the usual clink of beakers and noise of people gossiping there was silence. Sandy heard nothing from the dining-room, because there was another mid-morning gossip being carried on in the kitchen. He finished the word "recusancy" and wondered what it meant. Then Trevithic came down looking for him, and brought him up to the dining-room.

"We're all here now, are we?" said Mr Ardent. "Well, I think I shall have to ask what all this is about.

Shall we have a discussion privately first, Trevithic, or do you know as little as I do?"

"I know hardly anything, sir," said Trevithic. "Only what I found over there. If you ask them they'll tell you."

"I see," said Mr Ardent. "We'll have a general inquiry into the whole matter. This sounds like being a serious affair."

"Not me, sir, please." said the probationer with the pencil.

"You can run along," said Mr Ardent. "We shan't want you. You others stop grinning. Stand up: this is a serious affair, as I have already told you. Shall we have your side of it first, Trevithic?"

CHAPTER 7

Judgement Speaks

"I think it started yesterday, sir," said Trevithic. He went on to explain about the extra practice he had arranged with Dr Sunderland.

"Decani only?" asked Mr Ardent.

"At the beginning, yes, sir," said Trevithic. "But one of the singing boys told me this morning that Madington was going to capture the practice room for

Cantoris before we got there, so I decided not to have a Decani practice this morning."

"And told Decani so, I suppose?" said Mr Ardent.

"They all knew, sir," said Lowell. "I told them myself."

"Fact one," said Mr Ardent. "They all knew they hadn't to go. Now, Madington, what was your idea?"

Madington tucked Stanhope's handkerchief into his left sleeve, in case he needed it quickly. He was much saddened and upset by the events of the morning, but he answered clearly.

"I presumed that it would be a good victory, or joke, over Trevithic, sir," he said. "But I didn't expect them to behave like that."

"You thought Trevithic would be there to declare who had won and to keep order?" said Mr Ardent.

"I thought it would be easy to win," said Madington. "I thought of the idea first, but Trevithic got to Dr Sunderland first."

"We thought of it separately," said Trevithic. "But I tricked Madington yesterday."

"And what happened in the Cathedral today?" said Mr Ardent. "Why did Decani go across at all, and what were they doing when you got over there, Trevithic?"

"Madington was there first, sir," said Trevithic, who felt he had not been there long nor needed to do much when he was there.

"I got there first," said Madington. "I thought that Trevithic was before me, because Decani people were there as well; but both sides were going up the steps, so I went up too, to see whether we had lost or won. Two people were fighting, sir, in the doorway at the top."

"Who were they?" said Mr Ardent. "Hands up." Two hands went up. Mr Ardent looked at the two owners: every head turned to see who they were. "Two choristers," said Mr Ardent after a little while. His voice made the words mean "This is unutterable shame!" "But that is not all, I gather."

"No, sir," said Madington. "I went up and tried to stop them, and said that Cantoris could come up. But Decani wouldn't let them."

"Who in particular was responsible for that?" said Mr Ardent.

"All of us, sir," said Owen, a very young singing boy.

"I found them blocking the stairs," said Trevithic. "But not fighting. There was only one person fighting on the stairs, sir, and nobody was fighting back at him."

"I was, sir," said Stanhope, and stood like a vanquished and shamed angel.

"He was trying to send them all down again," said Trevithic. "The others were Decani and Cantoris – enemies – but he was trying to keep order."

"And what were you doing, Madington?" said Mr Ardent.

"Separating the people who were fighting in the practice room," said Madington. "But they wouldn't separate."

"And you, Trevithic, brought them all back?"

"Yes, sir," said Trevithic. "They wouldn't obey Madington, because he was at the top and they couldn't hear him. I told them to line up, one by one: it was easy: Lowell was with me, too."

"That seems to give me the details of a most disgraceful scene," said Mr Ardent. "If Trevithic had not fortunately realized that you might be acting foolishly, and come to stop you, where would the scene have ended? I shall have to take severe measures against the principal offenders, and I shall deal harshly with the others. Now Decani, why did you go to the Cathedral at all?"

Decani looked round at each other, and then at Trevithic. "They're looking at you," Mr Ardent told him.

"Not my orders, sir," said Trevithic. "Lowell had told them not to go, and I didn't say anything else."

Sandy, behind the rest at the back of the room, knew who it was they wanted: him. He had told them to go, but that he could be blamed for anything else that happened was not fair: he had carefully arranged with Silverman that Cantoris should not go. In that case, if Silverman said nothing about his reasons for not telling Cantoris to stay away, there was no call for Sandy to get himself into trouble by admitting something not entirely his own responsibility.

"Who told Decani to go to the practice room?" said Mr Ardent.

Sandy felt his cocoa harden into a lump inside him. But to speak would be to blame Silverman for not keeping his side of the bargain. Or had he spoken to Cantoris, and had they still decided to join battle? The cocoa rolled itself round once and went into a heavy sleep.

"Somebody knows," said Mr Ardent. "Who was it?"

The cocoa woke and jumped. Sandy saw the immediate future like a black wall all round him. The "most disgraceful affair" was *his* fault: *he* had made it happen. He felt the sweat run down his ribs, and the heat of confession gathered in his head. "I did it," he said.

"I see," said Mr Ardent. "I'm not surprised to find you at the bottom of it, Sandwell. You'd better go and wait in the hall, and I'll see you shortly."

"Yes, sir," said Sandy. He went out of the room. As he went, he heard Mr Ardent saying: "You'd all better have your cocoa, while I talk to Trevithic and the prefects. Stay in here, and no talking. You are all in disgrace."

That was the last Sandy heard of what went on in the dining-room. He walked down the passage, across the second-form room, and into the hall, and waited there. The sympathetic blue sky in the high windows sharpened the distress of his captivity. He looked away from it, and waited in the quiet, gazing at the bottom knob of the banisters: it was round and soothing and sensible. He tried for a moment to read the newspaper that lay on the rug where Trevithic had left it, but he found that the words meant nothing to his eyes. What if tomorrow's headlines said "Riot in Cathedral. Choristers fight in Treasury. Ringleader punished"? Punished: yes, punished was the word. How would it be done? Were ringleaders sent home, expelled? The round banister knob said nothing, but sat like a little yellow still world comfortably asleep.

There was no noise but the sound of the staff in the sitting-room upstairs, drinking their tea, and a sewing machine whirring in the linen room.

Mr Ardent came through from the study. While he spoke to Sandy he changed out of his cassock into his jacket, and pulled up his tie, which he had slacked off when he put on his clerical collar.

As Sandy listened, it became clearer and clearer that the cane was to be used. But that thought was not the one that mattered: the cane is a sting, but the words before are a consuming fire that smoulders a full term or more, and the slightest draught of a word can bring the words to red furnace rage, so that you are burnt seven times by the same blaze. The blazing started now. Sandy found first that his mouth began to tighten and his cheeks to move; then his nose began to want blowing, but he sniffed quietly. All at once he knew he was crying and that was not sensible. Yet, as soon as he felt the tears on his cheek he felt stronger and more sure, as though they had doused some of the fire. For one thing, he had been wanting to cry ever since he saw Madington in tears: he had realized more and more that Madington's tears were his own fault, and that he ought to have been weeping them.

Mr Ardent took no notice of the tears. He went on telling Sandy what sort of mistakes he was making by acting as if he had no duties or responsibilities.

"We are only here to do one thing: sing the Cathedral services, and that amounts, in the end, to taking care in everything we do. I know that you are trying to find out what sort of a person you are, and what kinds of things you can do; but, strange though it seems, the best way of becoming a real person, a real Peter Sandwell different from everybody else, is to forget yourself, and join with all your heart and soul in doing the job we are supposed to do: singing."

Sandy began to argue against this in his mind; surely it was as good a thing to be a singing boy as a chorister?

But before he could tell himself much, or Mr Ardent could say more, Silverman appeared from the second-form room.

"I'm afraid I'm busy, Silverman," said Mr Ardent.

"I know, sir," said Silverman. "But I remembered something about Cantoris."

"Yes?" said Mr Ardent, in his most unhelpful voice.

"I didn't tell them not to go to the practice room," said Silverman.

"Why should you have told them anything of the sort?" said Mr Ardent.

"We wanted a Decani practice, sir," said Silverman. "But Trevithic wanted a Cantoris one."

"So you thought you'd change it?" said Mr Ardent. "You two between you."

"Yes, sir," said Sandy.

"But I forgot about telling Cantoris," said Silverman. "And I've only just remembered."

"A little late now," said Mr Ardent. "But you have done some good by remembering: if I had gone on thinking that Sandwell was entirely to blame, I should have caned him."

"It was a mistake, sir," said Silverman.

"It was a bad, foolish mistake, all the way through," said Mr Ardent. "You have been silly, rather than wicked. You have been very thoughtless, and thoughtlessness does not pay. Go away now, both of you, and remember that the whole school has had to be punished for your folly, and that if they deal with you in their own way, you will get no sympathy from me. And the whole affair is to be forgotten as soon as possible: no talking about it at any time."

"No, sir," said Silverman in an agreeing sort of way, because he had already heard Mr Ardent say so.

Mr Ardent went back into the study, and came out a moment later to tell Silverman to ring the bell for the end of break. Sandy blew his nose and dried his face, and followed Silverman out of the hall.

CHAPTER 8

A Proud Walker

Twice during the afternoon Sandy's thoughts spun round again to Mr Ardent's talk – each time they sang the fourth verse of the afternoon's psalm, where ministers are called a flaming fire, he remembered the talk as if it were white ash, with the hot embers below.

"Sing 'mph out," said Dr Sunderland. "Being as exact as 'mph collection 'mph grandmas, but as cheerful as a lost sheep. C'm on, enjoy 'mph."

Nobody felt cheerful, nobody felt that the psalm

fitted the day at all: glorifying God and praising the excellence of the earth's creatures (in thirty-five verses) did not adequately commemorate the morning's troubles.

"Whadder'mph matter?" said Dr Sunderland to himself. "Too much dinner'mph."

At the end of practice he asked Trevithic how he had done at break. Trevithic was ready for the question, and to avoid answering it he asked another one back, about some of the harmony in the anthem. Trevithic could do that sort of thing to most people without offending them.

"'Mph," said Dr Sunderland, meaning "so it didn't go very well," and gave Sandy a long guessing look, which seemed like a poker in the embers of the morning's reproof.

The rest of the week walked by slowly, with nothing to help it on its way. There was no free time; there was no talking at meals. At break, Trevithic might have done what he liked, because the trouble was not his fault, but he took his share of marching everybody round the grass plot called the Oaks, the corner of the precincts where the grass could be used by the choir school: there was a notice to say so.

In the evening there might have been a little spare time, but even then no one was allowed to talk: the idea was more Trevithic's than Mr Ardent's. Mostly the time was spent in making the classrooms and the desks and lockers exquisitely clean, and checking up with Madington, who kept the stationery, that all the textbooks were whole and clean, and that each exercise book had all its pages.

Sandy found himself left alone in all this

investigation: even the tidying up of the music room, which he was supposed to look after and had never touched, brought no remarks, either from Trevithic, who was himself careful about music and instruments, and expected you to be as well, or from Madington, who should have seen that Sandy had done his job.

Lowell said nothing about Sandy's secretly modified bicycle, with the wheels changed round so that the chain drove the front one and you steered by leaning over. Lowell was Minister of Transport, and unable to allow bicycles to be used unless they were in good standard order, but after looking at the invention and the damage it had done to the front forks, he made no entry in his book and gave no orders to put it right.

By Saturday, Sandy began to notice in other ways that he was treated differently from the rest. When he fell out of line at break on Friday, to tie a shoelace again, Trevithic first said: "Hurry up, Sandwell," and then, when Sandy more or less accidentally broke the lace and delayed, Trevithic said "Join us when you're ready, unless you've got other things to do."

"Sorry, Trevithic," said Sandy, hurrying with the lace.

"I mean, you needn't march unless you want to," said Trevithic. "No reason for you to."

"I'll watch," said Sandy, wondering whether that was too bold an idea.

"That'll be all right," said Trevithic, and went off after the marchers. Sandy shifted the lace down one eyelet each side, and stood on the grass watching the marchers. That was interesting on Friday, but on Saturday it seemed boring and lonely, and unfair to the others, particularly to Stanhope, so he joined in:

61

pointless though the marching was, it had at least the merit of being accompanied by the rest of the school.

Saturday afternoon was devoted to country dancing, because the rain drizzled from dinner-time onwards, only stopping in a contrary way during service. Trevithic and Mr Lewis played the piano, taking it in turns, because they exhausted themselves inventing variations on the tunes: the same tune over and over again exactly the same is not very interesting. Towards the end, though, they performed a magnificent duet for "Gathering Peascods", and when the dance should have ended they were still racing their fingers up and down the keyboard, blowing the dust out of the piano, and being unable to stop because they were in quite the wrong key, or, more accurately, the wrong two keys. Peascods were gathered again, and they ended all together as the supper bell rang.

Mr Ardent came into the dormitory on Sunday morning to wake Trevithic and Madington to go to early service. Before Trevithic went downstairs he said, "The trouble is finished with: you can talk today as usual."

"Thank goodness for that," said Kelsey, who had been unable to pick quarrels with anyone, without the use of words.

There was extra time in bed on Sunday mornings. Sandy wrote his weekly letter then. If you only talked the time seemed wasted and stolen from the day, instead of added to it.

At breakfast, which was a talking meal again, Sandy found himself without marmalade: the dish was empty, a thing that sometimes happened if there was a miscalculation in the kitchen. Sandy asked Mr Lewis whether he could borrow some from another table.

"You can *try*," said Mr Lewis. "But it looks as if they've eaten it *all*."

Sandy scouted, and found that the slow-eating much-talking probationers had plenty of marmalade. He asked to borrow it; they all looked at their plates and said nothing. Sandy took the marmalade, helped himself to a spoonful and took it back. The probationers still said nothing; they were talking among themselves twice as fast as anyone else could go. Sandy said "Thank you" to them, but they did not hear. He went back to his place thinking that they ought to have taken some notice of a senior, especially of one who was better off than the others, considering that he had not been so much punished as they had. Perhaps that was due to his being Peter Sandwell rather than to his innocence. He had more or less caused the recent trouble, and only not been punished because he was better thought of than he felt.

He felt slightly superior when he went back to his table. The others had said their separate graces and gone; he was alone. His marmalade had gone too, and there was none of it on the plate.

"Licked off," said Sandy. "Jealous." It was the sort of chiz any table might practise on anyone. He ate the bread without marmalade, said his grace (with a reservation that "What we have received" would have been more strongly meant with marmalade) and went out.

He still felt slightly superior, having inspired jealousy in the others, so he whistled in the passage, which was against the rule, and went out to the Oaks in his house-shoes, which was just as much against the rule; but the thinner soles felt the ground better, nearly as well as bare feet, and without the sharp dangers of thorn and spiky beech mast.

There were visitors in the precincts already, looking at the Cathedral from the outside. There were many more during the summer; but every fine day in winter they walked in the precincts. Sandy straightened his jacket, his best Sunday one, and walked loftily and as if he were busy but not hurried. The trouble is, if you look to see whether the visitors are watching they never are; and if you don't look they are still as likely not to be watching.

The rest of the school on the Oaks seemed busy in itself. Some sat on a low garden wall in the sun, writing their letters. The juniors raced model cars on the asphalt, and the early day-boys circled slowly on their bicycles talking to each other about town things that boarders scarcely heard of. The people who were not busy took no notice of him when he came to them; and when he entered the conversation he was disregarded. He thought it must be a private talk, so he moved on to the letter-writers, who were now addressing their envelopes. Why did their writing on envelopes always seem much more real than his own?

He walked away from the talkers who had seemed not to notice him, but one of them said: "He's got his house-shoes on." There was a prefect there, Lowell, who might have said something about it, but he only remarked, "Let him do what he likes," in the tone of one repeating a rule rather than making a decision.

"Why can I do what I like?" thought Sandy. "People don't generally."

When he got to the letter-writers, they turned away

and talked to each other, but not sensibly: only in order to take no notice of him. He sat down beside the end one, Paterson, who got up at once, said to Meedman, "Let's go and look at something," and went away with Meedman following.

"Jealous," said Sandy, feeling more superior than ever, but a little doubtful as well. He looked at his shoes, shook his head slightly, as if he had just noticed that they were the wrong shoes, and walked slowly back to school with both hands in his pockets, not daring to look round in case the others were watching and smirking.

CHAPTER 9

In the Wilderness

Sandy found himself during the rest of the day left alone, and no one spoke a word to him. If he spoke to them, they walked off or imagined they did not see him. But, apart from the one remark about house-shoes, when he was on the Oaks, not a word was spoken behind his back, nor was he jeered at by gesture or manner: they did not smile secretly about him.

He thought, as the day went by, that it must be a sort of jealousy on their part, probably invented by Trevithic. He sang the morning's psalms with attention, because day by day in them there was something encouraging or discouraging: they were a kind of holy horoscope. Today the godly man was not afraid for any evil tidings; the ungodly saw it and was grieved, gnashed his teeth, and consumed away. That was a help, and seemed to confirm that the others were jealous of something; but when the psalms were over, the loneliness of being ignored came back, and Sandy felt that the words of no known psalm would fit the case, though David, who wrote them all, had been an outlaw and the king his enemy.

The afternoon's psalms were much more to the point. They began to cheer Sandy in practice. Talking about idols, the psalm said: "They have mouths and speak not: eyes have they and see not. They have ears and hear not: noses have they and smell not. They have hands and handle not; feet have they and walk not: neither speak they through their throats."

"Why'mph grinning, Sandwe'mph?" said Dr Sunderland.

"At the psalm, sir," said Sandy, but he could not explain how he likened the rest of the school to the idols of the heathen, so he said "Toes have they, sir, and tootle not."

"'Mph," said Dr Sunderland, meaning "Old joke". But Cantoris smiled at the improvement, and began to invent other ideas, until Madington, seeing Trevithic glare, stopped them, and the practice went on. Stanhope edged a paper into Sandy's hand. It said: "Shut up or they'll make it worse."

Sandy waited until the end of the practice, and said loudly, dropping the note on the floor, "I don't care."

"Yes, you do," said Trevithic. "Pick it up."

Sandy left it, however, and Stanhope picked it up. Sandy wished it had been Trevithic being made to tidy up after others, but all in all he considered he was showing his independence well: he did not mind what they thought.

His comfort lasted until the end of the psalms during service: the last verse but one said "The dead praise not thee, O Lord: neither all they that go down into silence." During practice he thought "they that go down into silence" meant the ones who kept silence, but now it seemed that he might be the one that had gone down.

After tea there was unrestricted free time, as usual:

all last week's restrictions had vanished. Sandy was brought in by Mr Lewis, who took no notice of privately-arranged silences, to play Mah-Jongg with Silverman and Lowell, who were clever players. Mr Ardent played bridge with Trevithic, Madington and Kelsey.

Sandy found himself under a slight handicap in the game, because the other two would allow him no help: generally a better player would tell you what pieces to discard, and what to build up with, making the game more difficult for themselves but more interesting for the rest. Today, if Sandy made a small mistake (very likely under the five-second rule they played to), he was left alone, and confused himself entirely. He was left with the head and tail of a Wriggling Snake, with nothing but West Winds and "bars of soap" to fill the middle. Mr Lewis was no better a player. Mr Ardent was the cunning expert; without him Mr Lewis and Sandy lost every round, and Sandy wished he had not started to play. When Silverman and Madington went to sing the 6.30 service, Sandy left the table too, in case juniors came to play and witness his ineptitude.

He went downstairs to read in his classroom, because, when he went to the day-room, where the comfortable chairs were, no one would answer his knock and let him in: you had to have permission to enter.

He was still reading when the whistle blew for supper duty patrol to lay the tables and bring in the food. He was senior on duty tonight, and he went to supervise, thinking out a joke on "supperwise" and "supervise"; but when he got there all the work had been arranged among the juniors by themselves and left him nothing to do, and no way of doing anything either, because they would not hear what he said. They would not even help him race the trolley across the floor, which was the best part of the prefectless Sunday supper duty patrol.

At supper, Kelsey, real head of the duty patrol now, served second helpings, but to Sandy he gave none, and ignored his empty plate. Sandy, in revenge on everybody, refilled the teapot with water from the wrong kettle, and brought it back chill; and as no tea could be left by anyone, the second-tea-ers had to drink it cold, with the sugar unmelted in the bottoms of the beakers. But no one said anything. Monday morning came with bright sun on the dormitory wall, but in the moment of waking Sandy remembered the heavy silence he was in all day. The time by Meedman's watch on the locker was twenty past seven. Sandy decided to get up ten minutes early, so that by missing the crowds he would not so much feel their disdain.

He was washing when Trevithic followed him into the bathroom. Sandy took no notice: silence could serve both sides.

"We shan't speak to you until you mend your ways," said Trevithic. "We're tired of you being such an idiot and not behaving properly. If you don't improve, we shall keep you in Coventry for the rest of the term, and if you get any worse we shall do something different. It isn't only what you did on Thursday; it's the way you act generally, swearing and swanking, and being a nuisance."

Sandy washed his ears, to drown Trevithic's voice, dried them with a great deal of towel, cleaned his teeth, spat, splashed about the water in the basin, hung up his towel on its hook by one corner, not the loop, pushing Trevithic aside to do it, and went back into the dormitory in a black rage whistling. As soon as he was in the middle of the room, the others all sat up and threw their slippers at him, and lay down again pretending to be asleep.

Twenty slippers at half past seven in the morning would stop any whistle. They had not hurt or bruised him: they increased his rage so much that he would, if he had dared, have thrown all the slippers out of the window into the precincts, but that was beyond doing. He dressed, and left the dormitory, stepping over the scattered slippers between the beds.

He went out of the school and into the Cathedral, up the worn steps into the north-east transept: to stay in school would be to see the others too soon, and to go on to the Oaks would allow them to watch him. At first he was not miserable but angry, but when he was tempted to show his anger and tried to slam the Cathedral doors, they would not bang but sank slowly with a slight hiss: he used the energy of his rage trying to hurry the door into its doorway, and found the calm resistance of the door a good rage-queller.

His rage gone, he felt light and joyful, alone in the great warm building, with only the Treasury clock to measure the idea of time. He walked in the newly springing sunlight among the tombs of saints, kings and princes.

But as he walked the sun went cold behind a cloud, and left the bright windows dull and the inner arches in shadow. Sandy's quick cheerfulness passed away and his loneliness came back to him. He felt hungry, too, so he went down to the Treasury to look at the clock and not be late for breakfast.

"What are you doing?" said Turle, who was there with a box in his hand locking the door of the inner Treasury.

"Walking about to look at the time," said Sandy.

"Getting on for breakfast," said Turle.

"Another quarter of an hour," said Sandy. "That's all."

"Don't you want your breakfast?" said Turle: Sandy's voice had sounded sad. "Never pleased with what's there, you boys."

"Breakfast's all right," said Sandy. "But the rest of the school are foul."

Turle had been unlocking the door of the Treasury again. "You can save me five minutes," he said, "by taking this to the Chapter workshop: they won't have opened the door yet, but they'll be there. Put it outside: there's a note in it."

"Oh, all right," said Sandy, wondering whether Turle had any right to ask him to do things.

"No need to groan," said Turle. "Do it or don't."

"I will," said Sandy. "I wasn't thinking about that."

"I heard there was some nonsense the other day," said Turle. "Den of thieves. Lucky for you I wasn't there."

"My fault, almost," said Sandy, finding that to tell even Turle about it was a help. "Mr Ardent's let us off now, but nobody will speak to me."

"Hmn," said Turle, and, as usual, quoted from the day's psalms: " 'The Lord hath chastened and corrected me: but he hath not given me over unto death,' so what can you complain about, hey?"

"Everything," said Sandy, and took the box away.

He went out through the cloisters. He found that the box held a broken wooden bookstand belonging to one of the side chapels. He took it to the Chapter workshop under the twin western towers, and left it there. On the way out of the workshops he saw two dustbins: the Cathedral had them, like any other house, and hanging over the edge of one was his conker chain on a 'cello string. He took it, and on his way through the cloisters he hid it behind the carved top of an arcade, where it lay invisible to all but giants, like a brown caterpillar of previously unknown length.

CHAPTER 10

Friends Outside

Sandy came back to school as the second bell rang for breakfast. He washed his hands and walked in late to his porridge. He apologized to Mr Ardent for unpunctuality.

"I had to go the Chapter workshop for Turle, sir."

"I see," said Mr Ardent. "All right, sit down."

Sandy went to sit down, working out in his head a

plan to defeat the others. He had noticed the interest in their looks when he talked about the Chapter workshop. It ought to be quite simple, he thought, to make them all so curious that they would be bound to ask questions and speak to him and want to know things; and the way to make them so was to have a busy look and seem to be intent on other things. Perhaps they would feel themselves in Coventry more than he.

He thought of two things he could immediately go off and do. One was to collect his conkers, and the other to visit the workshop and see whether the bookrest was ready. He ate his breakfast quickly, and was out of the room among the first, having been greedy over the marmalade without being reproached. He carefully recombed and parted his hair, looked to see that he was tidy, took his cap, and went out of doors. There was no need to wear a cap in the precincts, but it added to the mystery of what he was doing and where he was going.

He went through the Dark Entry and to the cloisters, imagining to himself that he was going out on some important school business. He knew it was not so, but it was pleasant to think himself free for a time, and useful to somebody.

There was no one about to beware of, so he walked the long way round the cloisters, two and a half sides instead of one and a half, glancing at the conkers on the way, and making a long conversation in which everybody else admitted their inabilities, and he put them right and forgave them for their unkindnesses.

By the time he came out of the cloisters he felt so much the man that he would, if he had met him at the Palace gates, have nodded to the Bishop instead of raising his cap. But no Bishop was there. There was only the eldest Pargale in the next gateway, which belonged to the Chapter workshop.

There were three Pargales in the Chapter workshop, working for the Cathedral. There was a fourth Pargale, too, who would be working there in the years to come, and a fifth who had worked there in the years gone by. The youngest of them had been christened during the summer, with four singing boys to hide his shrieks. The other Pargales were his great-great-grandfather, retired; his great-grandfather, standing in the gateway now; his grandfather; and his father: ever since the Cathedral had stood a Pargale had worked there.

"We've nussed her up from being no more than a chapel," eldest Pargale would say. "She's our only daughter: we don't run to 'em otherwise, us Pargales. We can see her breathe, and we don't reckon many can do that."

When Sandy approached, eldest Pargale looked up from his standing still and said: "Are you for the book-rest?"

"If it's ready," said Sandy.

"Eleven o'clock," said eldest Pargale. "And tell young Turle we didn't make it for to be played cricket against."

"I will," said Sandy.

"Dad," said middle Pargale (the baby's grandfather) from the open mid-air door in the wall above. "Ask him does he want shavings?"

"Bound to be he does, Son," said eldest Pargale. "But they took two sacks."

"Thought so, Dad," said middle Pargale. "Let 'em

fill as often as they want for."

"Dad," said youngest Pargale (the baby's father) from the back of the shop, "let him see what he wants."

"I will, Son," said middle Pargale. "Let him up, Dad."

"He's coming up, Son," said eldest Pargale.

They always arranged matters between them before telling you what they had decided; and they always repeated instructions and warnings, after a long habit of making certain everybody on a scaffolding or a pinnacle knew what was about to happen.

Sandy went up the narrow stairs to the wood-working shop. It was full of precincts staircases, doors, chests, beams, and all the good wood saved from any alterations since there had been any buildings to be altered; as well as being full already of new wood. In clear spaces were things being made: rails for a chapel, new doors for the library, a desk to display postcards, and a big cupboard for vestments, to go in the Treasury, so large that before it could be got out, the shop would have to be emptied.

In a corner, beside a mechanical plane for smoothing planks, there was a heap of wood-shavings, sawdust and offcuts, enough to fill three or four sacks.

"Yours to take," said youngest Pargale.

"He can have it, Son," said middle Pargale.

"Take it in his own sacks," said eldest Pargale. "Save us the burning."

"Thank you," said Sandy. "What we can't get inside the guy we can put on the fire itself."

"As soon as he can, Dad," said youngest Pargale.

"It's wanted out of the way, Dad," said middle Pargale.

"Take it early, Dad," said eldest Pargale. He often called people "Dad", out of habit; though his own father was still alive in the town, sitting, it was said, in a chair by a window, watching the Cathedral towers, having sworn to watch day and night until he died; and having forgotten to die was still watching.

"We will collect it," said Sandy.

"He can wheel it, Son," said eldest Pargale.

"He won't need sacks if he takes the trucks, Son," said middle Pargale.

"He can wheel it on the handcart," said youngest Pargale.

"He can't lose that, Dad."

"No," said the other Pargales in turn.

Sandy thanked them again, and said he would come back at eleven for the bookrest, and borrowed a piece of brown paper from them. All four agreed on a piece, and Sandy took it, nodded at young, smiled at middle, and raised his cap to eldest; they winked at each other, pleased at such well-graded politeness, and Sandy went away.

The brown paper was for the conkers. He laid the paper down on the stone that said "Sometime Dean of this Cathedral Church", brought down the conkers, coiled them up and wrapped them, tucked the parcel under his arm, and walked back to school as Trevithic rang the bell for practice.

Sandy had chosen his time well, and he knew that no one would be in the dormitories, so he broke a rule and went up there, tiptoeing the spiral staircase, and put the parcel in his bedside locker, breaking another rule by having such things there. He came safely down, and walked across to practice five seconds after the rest, forgetting he was in Coventry, and wondering how to keep possession of the Pargales' wood shavings and force the others to ask him for them.

In the Cathedral there was little talking at any time, so the affliction of silence was not felt. Turle was in the Treasury when they began to file up to the practice room. He looked along the line for Sandy, so Sandy went to him: he thought that any mention of the Chapter workshop should be made out of hearing of the others, in case they thought about wood-shavings.

"I'll get it at eleven o'clock," said Sandy.

"Today?" said Turle. "'Marvellous in our eyes'."

"They say you mustn't use it for cricket again," said Sandy.

"Who said?" said Turle.

"Eldest Pargale," said Sandy. "A joke, I think."

"Old him," said Turle. "No repeating that among you boys, mind."

Sandy left Turle to think of a threat, and followed Owen towards the steps. Dr Sunderland came behind him, thumped his ribs with a great hand that should have been born on a gorilla rather than a human, and said: "Stretched 'mph lungs?"

"Bit, sir," said Sandy.

"Sat'day," said Dr Sunderland. "That'mph day. Nobody done a stroke so far'mph. How's 'mph theory going, 'mph?"

"Theory test as well, sir?" said Sandy, who thought he got along well enough without theory, and had not for a moment imagined that the chorister's test was more than singing.

"'Mph course," said Dr Sunderland. "Can't judge on noise, Sandwe'mph."

"No, sir," said Sandy, and vanished himself up the staircase quickly to think, because while Dr Sunderland spoke it had dawned on him that practically the only way to get himself out of silence before the end of term was to become a chorister on Saturday. But he knew that if musical theory was to be considered as well, then there was no chance at all, unless he learnt everything he should have learnt since becoming a singing boy.

Considering the ordinary difficulties of the musical theory he knew already, it seemed to him that somebody would have to help, and how could that be.

"Perhaps I know more than I think," he thought. "But I can't, or I should know that I did. Plainsong, for instance ... "

Dr Sunderland put himself sideways and crab-walked up to the practice room last of the line, came into the room, and said "Open the windows."

CHAPTER 11

Theory

All through practice Sandy thought, and the ideas that came into his head were: "Trevithic will leave before I do, and when he does, somebody ought to know as much about music as he does: ought we all to know so much?" and the thought that followed it: "How much are we supposed to know?" It seemed to him that Trevithic's knowledge might be unusual, and more than ordinary people might have. But he thought again that it might not be so when Trevithic asked a question about some matter of cadences, very obscure to Sandy, who had never paid attention to them. Dr Sunderland seemed not to be sure of his answer, and waited for people to put up their hands.

"Stanhope," said Dr Sunderland. Stanhope had had a thought about passing-notes.

"No," said Dr Sunderland, and Sandy waited for all the others to be wrong as well: surely only Trevithic had the slightest idea about it?

"Change to key of the mediant, sir," said Meedman.

Sandy had a private thought that Meedman had gone mad and named the non-existent.

"Look at 'mph," said Dr Sunderland. "Whadder'mph, key of mediant?"

"I didn't see the change of clef, sir," said Meedman, looking again.

Sandy felt a sudden alarm. What if Meedman *did* know about such things? Why had Sandy forgotten them? What if only Sandy were left a singing boy, after the test, because he was not good enough, instead of because he did not *want* to be a chorister? How could it possibly be true that Meedman, his junior, knew more? Surely it could not happen?

But it seemed to be: even Paterson said something about sub-dominants, and Dr Sunderland said "Ye'mph,"

Paterson was astonished: he had said it as a guess, but for all that, he did know what a sub-dominant was. Dr Sunderland gave Trevithic an explanation of the harmony at that point in the music, and the practice went on.

At the end, while the rest went down to the vestry to put on surplices, Sandy stayed for a moment to ask Dr Sunderland for a book on theory. "What about 'mph notes you've made with Mr Lewis?" said Dr Sunderland.

"Not very good ones, sir," said Sandy.

"H'mph," said Dr Sunderland, meaning "It's all very well to admit it, but it ought never to have been so." He looked among the books on a window-ledge, and found one called *An Exposition of Musical Theory* and gave it to Sandy, who put it under his cassock and followed the others to the vestry.

He put the book on the floor of his locker: it was not the sort of thing that would be confiscated or put in the Cathedral dustbin. He left it with the title upwards, so that anybody seeing it might leave it alone, and so that Trevithic might begin to feel that Sandy was not altogether lacking in responsibility towards the choir. The book showed that there was an improvement in his behaviour, Sandy thought, and, more than that, it was an improvement Trevithic had not mentioned in the bathroom early in the morning.

"Lead on," said Trevithic, when they were all in surplices. Stanhope closed the locker doors that were accidentally left open. He saw the *Exposition of Musical Theory*, read the title, and looked at Sandy in a very friendly and satisfying way. Sandy returned the look with a smile, and followed Stanhope to the Treasury. Was the silence at last breaking?

At eleven o'clock Sandy drank his cocoa among the first, waited a few moments more for Stanhope to appear, but in vain, and went off to the Chapter workshop.

"For young Turle's bookrest, Son," said eldest Pargale to middle Pargale.

"For Turle's bookrest, Son," said middle Pargale to

youngest Pargale.

"For old Turle's bookrest, Dad," said youngest Pargale, bringing the mended bookrest in its box. "What's the boy say about those shavings, Dad?"

"Did he say, Dad?" said middle Pargale.

"Did you, Dad?" said eldest Pargale to Sandy.

"I didn't, yet," said Sandy. "But I will. Don't let the others have them, will you? I don't think we know where the fire can be."

The three Pargales thought it might be in an empty plot of ground at number 13, where a vanished precincts house had stood.

"Dad heard," said youngest Pargale.

"Dad told *me*," said middle Pargale.

"Young Turle heard from Canon Fredley," said eldest Pargale.

"But where he heard from I can't say, Son."

"He don't think much of such larks," said youngest Pargale.

"And *I* told him it was 13, likely."

"Son said so, Dad," said middle Pargale.

"So it will be, Dad," said eldest Pargale to Sandy. "We used to dangle squibs off her top tower, but the idee's gone. I done it, Son didn't."

"It would be a good idea," said Sandy. "Why can't we?"

"No sparrow-hawks, Dad," said eldest Pargale.

"Too many pigeons, messy birds, and daws, Dad," said middle Pargale.

"Too many nestses, Dad," said youngest Pargale. "Fire: don't want to burn her."

"Lost her all once or twice, Son," said middle Pargale.

"And parts here and there off her, Son," said eldest Pargale. "She's mostly left, though, Dad."

"She's very nice," said Sandy. "She's the best Cathedral."

"I seen good bits on others, mind, Dad," said eldest Pargale. "We'll work 'em in, one way and other."

Sandy thanked them for the bookrest, and for a precaution against anyone else who might think of taking the wood-shavings, told eldest Pargale his name, Peter Sandwell. Eldest Pargale handed the name down to youngest Pargale, who put it by to remember.

Turle was not in the Cathedral, but had gone across to his house to drink tea. Sandy saw him and followed him. Turle took the box, but said nothing because his mouth was full of scone diluted with tea. Sandy left him and walked the length of the precincts, thinking what to do next in order to appear busy.

The *Exposition of Musical Theory* was in his pocket, and he would have sat on a bench to read it, where he could look up on the Cathedral nave, but this part of the precincts was out of bounds to loiterers: you were supposed to walk through and by no means linger except to feed the pigeons, if you had anything for them.

Sandy went back to the school, into the empty building and to his desk. The rest of the school were on the Oaks: Sandy could see them through the window as he went to the desk. One person ran up to the Oaks as he watched: Paterson, looking back over his shoulder at the fourth form window.

The *Exposition* started in well-known territory, and at the end of break, after reading steadily through every word, Sandy had come across nothing he did not

THEORY

thoroughly know, but he had not read very far. When
the bell rang he put the book away. Somebody had been
at his desk: the books had been pulled away from the
edges and heaped in an untidy way over the middle. He
was looking at the haystack of books when Paterson
came in, looking at him with curiosity.

"Did you do this?" said Sandy.

Paterson looked round to see that no one else was
there.

"Yes," he said. "But don't tell anyone."

"I'll tell you," said Sandy. "And I don't care what
Trevithic says. You know you're not allowed in desks."
While he spoke he was thinking out a scientific attack:
he knew the usual way of grabbing and clinging on and
relying on weight produced no sort of a fight, even if
you were heavier. A weapon was the best advantage, so
he took the waste-paper basket and put it over
Paterson's head. Paterson tried to push it up, but
offered no fight.

"Honestly," he said, "I wish you would tidy your
desk."

"Brat," said Sandy, but before he could bring the
matter any further on he was seized from behind, and
had to leave the basket to attack his new opponent.

"I think," said a dry voice, "that even the most
valiant defence is foolhardy, Sandwell."

Mr Sutton. Sandy stopped punching blind and
turned round. "It was all right to fight, sir," he said.
"He's been at my desk."

"Go and sit down, Sandwell, and before you go to
dinner you will pick up the paper from the floor. Now,
today we deal with differences of gender in the second
declension . . . " and they went on to discuss the names

85

of trees.

In the middle of his desk Sandy found, holding up Kennedy's *Shorter Latin Primer* (altered to Eating primer) a little packet, which he opened during some second declension nouns ending in -us, but neuter, which was apparently unusual. The packet held four squares of chocolate, and on them was written "From a friend", and when Sandy looked up (ignoring Mr Sutton entirely for the moment) Paterson was watching, and Sandy felt ashamed of wanting to fight him.

"Why do you gape, Sandwell?" said Mr Sutton.

"Thinking, sir," said Sandy, looking at the book in a hurry.

"Wondering whether, sir" (hastily looking for something intelligent to say) "whether father-in-law had anything to do with football, sir. One's 'Socer' with one c, and the other's 'Soccer' with two c's."

CHAPTER 12

A Trial Watched

Sandy ate the four pieces of chocolate between lessons, and when he had the opportunity he said to Paterson:

"Sorry about the waste-paper basket."

There were too many people in the room for Paterson to risk answering and speak to an outlaw: he could only look, and looks mean anything, unless they are actual smiles. Sandy said, "Dark Entry afterwards," so that only Paterson would hear.

There was a little time between the end of school and dinner. Sandy did not feel the usual extreme pangs of hunger, because of the chocolate, so he was able to feel cheerful among the cooking smells. Paterson was hungry, and doubtful whether he should break Sandy's silence, but he came to the Dark Entry before deciding what to do.

"*You* can talk to me, I think," he told Sandy. "But *I'd* better not talk to you, or Trevithic will find out."

"What can he do?" said Sandy. "*I'm* not interested in him, if he turns people into enemies."

"Not all enemies," said Paterson. "Really, you know."

"Except you, of course," said Sandy. "Is anyone else

not an enemy?"

"Who do you mean?" said Paterson, knowing quite well that Sandy meant Stanhope. "*He* isn't an enemy."

"Good," said Sandy. "I can talk to him, and I don't care about the others. Except you."

"But don't talk to me," said Paterson making up his mind about how nearly he could break the silence rule. "Trevithic wouldn't like it."

"Chiz Trevithic," said Sandy. "I wish everyone was turned to stone, except me and Stanhope."

"I'm not your enemy, but I won't talk to you," said Paterson. "And I don't see why *I* should be a stone."

The dinner-bell rang, and Paterson hurried into the school, leaving Sandy wondering whether he had been unkind to the only sure friend he had. He found that he could have been more helpful and less argumentative. Perhaps another conversation would soothe Paterson, and lead him to carry messages to Stanhope, because Sandy himself hardly dare speak, in case Stanhope was not interested: the best Sandy could do was make jokes that Stanhope might laugh at.

There was no more opportunity to speak to Paterson during the day. In fact, he avoided Sandy. But Sandy had the other bother on his mind: the mastering of the *Exposition of Musical Theory*. He went slowly onwards through it, hiding the book when Trevithic came near, in case he approved of it: Sandy knew that learning was the right thing, but he did not want Trevithic to think that the putting-in-silence had forced him to it.

Tuesday morning brought breakfast duty patrol. Sandy came downstairs first, and took Mr Lewis a cup of tea. He complained of being woken *up* on a cold morning like *this*, until Sandy draped his dressing-gown over him and made sure he was strong enough to stir his tea. Sandy went down again to make the toast, and combined the business with reading again some *Lives of Great Composers*, which seemed to be part of theory; but why, when being born at such and such a time and dying at another scarcely seemed a musical exercise.

"Purcell, Henry, b. 1659, d. 1695" (an easy pair to remember) was as far as he could get during the toasting, and it was probably further than he could remember.

After breakfast, with the washing-up done, he broke rules again by walking off through a light drizzle to the cloisters and sitting on a stone ledge reading the *Exposition* until the rest of the choir went up to practice: he saw them along the dark length of the Entry and caught them up in the vestry after walking quickly through the Cathedral.

Stanhope was there now, but with no friendly glance this morning: he did not look at Sandy at all. Sandy thought that Paterson had been talking to him, but Paterson, feeling that his kindness yesterday had not helped, kept away.

Sandy's opportunity to speak came during practice. He managed to communicate with Stanhope without saying a word: he pointed out the 71st verse of the psalm, which said "It is good for me that I have been in trouble." Sandy did not feel strongly that it was true, but it would be approved, and he could always disagree again without changing his mind. When the psalm ended, at the next verse, Stanhope said "Yes, it is: if you don't forget."

"You can remind me," said Sandy.

"If you really mean it, I will," said Stanhope.

"Magnificat, Magnificat," said Dr Sunderland. "Stop talking, Sandwe'mph."

"Sorry, sir," said Sandy, anxious not to be corrected just as he was mending his ways, yet still pleased that Trevithic would think he was no better than he had been.

Stanhope, after his few words in public, would not talk in private, and Sandy, struggling with differences in time signatures (according to the *Exposition*) began to forget that his silence was not his own idea.

At dinner-time Mr Ardent called Sandy to him between courses, and explained something that he wanted done, "Or, rather," he said, "Dr Sunderland wants it. Will you go with Trevithic to the organ loft after service and act as look-out man during the Alto Lay Clerks' voice trial. Dr Sunderland has some candidates coming after service, and since he can't play the organ and listen to the singing, Trevithic will play, and you can watch Dr Sunderland and tell Trevithic when to stop and start."

"Yes, sir," said Sandy, pleased to be favoured and miss a lesson.

"You can do your prep after supper," said Mr Ardent, "so don't think yourself privileged: you're not, but there's the chorister's test on Saturday, and you might as well be given a reminder of what they're like, because it's high time you got somewhere in choir instead of being a troublesome junior."

"Yes, sir," said Sandy, and went to sit down again, with a new blaze in the ashes of last Thursday's lecture.

On the way he saw Lowell neatly evading blancmange, which he hated. The duty patrol had served the senior table first, and they had begun. Lowell, with a full plate before him, had sadly started on the jam, nibbling it from the spoon, when Madington, dishing out jam at the trolley, reminded Mr Lewis, in charge of the blancmange, of Lowell's hatred. Mr Lewis sent down an insect's helping; and Lowell found himself with two plates, one full with the jam eaten, and the other merely splashed with blancmange. The helpful member of the duty patrol had gone away without removing the first helping. Lowell shuffled the plates about, and seeing Mr Ardent talking to Trevithic, got up, pretended to be duty patrol himself, and handed the large helping to a junior, who ate it at once without asking questions. Lowell came back very pleased. "Remember what happened when I did eat it once?" he said.

"Please shut up, Lowell," said DeMaris. "Your table manners were not nice that day."

"Nor was the blank-wobble," said Lowell, scraping his spoon round and making the second plate look as if it had been eaten from.

Sandy took the *Exposition* with him to practice, and had it in his pocket when he and Trevithic went to the organ loft after service. The door in the choir screen was open, and the light was burning on top. Sandy and Trevithic went up, and found, not Dr Sunderland, but middle Pargale and Turle, both examining the top edges of some boards that stood upright against the piers of the tower and hid wires going down into the aisle.

"What are you doing?" said Turle. "No boys up

here."

"We're going to play the organ," said Trevithic. "By special request of the management."

"I shouldn't have left the door open," said Turle. "Down you go."

Trevithic switched on the electric blower and explained to Turle what they were doing.

"How does Dr Sunderland know that it's convenient?" said Turle. "Pargale wants to work up here."

"I don't hear noise," said middle Pargale.

"Thank you," said Trevithic. "Pargale III, isn't it?" How's Pargale I?"

"Dad's Dad?" said middle Pargale. "Well enough, watching harder than ever: fancies they'll be off with her one day. They'll be off with him before that, we reckon."

"You always reckon it'll fall down if you take your eyes off it," said Turle.

"We're always putting it up again," said middle Pargale. "It's what I'm doing now."

"Those boards always shake when Tweedledum really gets going," said Trevithic. "It's best to mend them. And how's Pargale II?" He went through the list of five Pargales and heard that they were all well, and by the time he had finished Dr Sunderland called up the staircase for the boys. Turle went down with them and back to the Treasury again.

"I thought of a joke," said Trevithic, when they had come up again full of instructions. He sounded one note to make sure the organ worked, and pulled out the stops he wanted. "The joke is," said Trevithic, "and you aren't to repeat it, that Tweedledee" (Turle)

"has just been spoiling Tweedledum's nice new rattle."

Sandy said "They'll resolve to have a battle," and went to look over the edge of the choir screen at Dr Sunderland below with the men who wanted to be

Alto Lay Clerks. Dr Sunderland gave him pre- arranged signals, and Sandy took them to Trevithic, who played the same two things twice for each Alto, continuing each time until Dr Sunderland sent a signal to Sandy.

Middle Pargale went on silently cutting and nailing, heedless of the music, as if he were a little live part of the Cathedral and not a man at all.

CHAPTER 13

Refusal and Acceptance

"Why do you talk to me?" said Sandy.

"I like talking," said Trevithic. He had had time to think of the answer, because Sandy had to go back to the edge of the choir screen after the question to watch Dr Sunderland.

"So do I," said Sandy, when next he came.

"We know that," said Trevithic, and Sandy went to think of the meanings in those three words. They engaged his mind so much that he forgot the *Exposition* lying there, though the fact that the test was going on below him ought to have been a reminder.

There was no more talk: Sandy was mostly away from the organ stool, and even when he was there he was so doubtful of Trevithic's attitude that he said nothing. Besides, Trevithic was thinking hard about playing, as well as being slightly troubled by middle Pargale working behind him.

At last Dr Sunderland signalled to Sandy that the test was over. Sandy brought the message to Trevithic.

"Slow ahead," said Trevithic. "Cut engines," and pushed all the stops in together by pressing a knob. Sandy switched off, and the needle of the pressure gauge stepped back to 0. Trevithic put out the keyboard and pedal lamps, pulled down the roll top, and locked the organ.

"Nearly five," he said. "And there's simply sheets of prep to do."

"And other things," said Sandy, meaning the *Exposition*.

"Do you think you'll be a chorister?" said Trevithic.

"Depends," said Sandy.

"It would be a good thing if you were," said Trevithic. "Good for Decani. You could be if you tried."

"Might," said Sandy, not wanting to decide publicly in case he failed.

"You'd want some help," said Trevithic. "You

aren't very famous in theory, are you?"

"Not very," said Sandy. "Time signatures seem a bit funny, and you want two people for the bit about triads, and there's a chapter about 'Form', and I don't know what that is."

"I'll help you with those," said Trevithic, "instead of those extra practices."

"No, thank you," said Sandy.

"Why?" said Trevithic.

"Because you're not trying to *help* me," said Sandy. "You're only doing it for Decani, and because you think you'll make me change, and I won't change for you, even if I stay in silence for a year."

"I expect you will, then," said Trevithic shortly, and went down from the organ loft. "I'll leave the door open," he said to middle Pargale. "But I'll close them all for you," he told Sandy. "You needn't expect me to speak to you until you are a chorister, and if you never are I never shall."

"Brat," said Sandy, and walked off alone, full of rage against people who tried to make you change your feelings.

The rest of the day was an extra lesson with Mr Ardent and the third-form French (which Sandy found he could just keep up with: why was French so forgettable?) and after supper the prep he should have done before. He did it alone in the dining-room, and made it last until bedtime, stormed upstairs in a great rush, and pretended to go to sleep as soon as he got into bed.

He woke up with a new idea, difficult to work, but putting everything the right way round. He would learn all the theory, every bit, and be able to ask

Trevithic-like questions, but he would fail to be a chorister, and instead set himself up as a worker in Stanhope's following, arranging the affairs of the school behind the prefects' backs, being careful not to rely on Silverman. Of course, the prefects would have to be brought into submission too, but there was a way of doing that. To start with, there was the bonfire, and the shavings for it and the guy, which he had in his charge: the question was, where to store them?

The answer came during breakfast. It meant going out of bounds, but that could be forgotten. When he had finished he went to the Chapter workshop, and after the usual three to one conversation, youngest Pargale brought out the two-wheeled truck used for carrying light things. Middle Pargale lent him a short shovel, and eldest Pargale, as a special mark of favour, provided him with a sack, "Which you've to bring back, Dad," he ordered.

Sandy filled the sack upstairs, dragged it down, emptied it into the truck, and went back for more, until the heap had gone and the truck was full. Then he wheeled the load across the precincts to number 13, opposite the choir transept on the south side, opened the gate, and went in, which was breaking the law.

There was a jungle here, and in the jungle the overturned broken stone out of the Cathedral: fractured columns and cracked capitals, worn knobs, chipped crockets, and dusty slices of arches, shapeless worn gargoyles, and fretted pinnacles, all lying under the year's dead grass and brown nettles. There were tree trunks here too, from forgotten trees, and one of the trunks was hollow, with a cavity large enough to take Sandy and Meedman, if feet and faces shared the same spaces: there was room for all the wood-shavings.

The Cathedral clock sounded the seven notes of half past eight. Sandy looked into the tree trunk to be sure it was empty: now it was a treasure chest, not Meedman's patent space rocket. There was nothing inside, so he charged it with shavings until the truck was empty, rolled a gaunt angel and a six-sided stone from a pillar against the opening, scattered a handful of leaves over the spilt whitewood scraps, and ran back to the workshop with the truck.

"All hurry here," said eldest Pargale, though he had only been looking at the ground as you might say slowly. "Always here and there, out of the way before a service starts, or in to finish something before it begins."

"It was made for services," said Sandy.

"They can't have them if it falls about their ears," said eldest Pargale.

Sandy gave him back the sack, the shovel, and the handcart. "Will you have any more before the fifth?" he asked.

"Don't reckon, Dad," said eldest Pargale.

"Not cutting, Dad," said middle Pargale.

"But we'll tell him or the tall one, Trevithic, if there is any, Dad," said youngest Pargale. So they all agreed, and Sandy thought the matter was best left like that, and that he would have to be about every day to get the message first. He ran to school, shaking the sawdust from his hair and clothes as he went.

He walked after a little way, not minding if he was late, to check that there was no trail of suspicious wood-shavings across the asphalt. The ground seemed clear of them: luckily the day was dull and windless. He was passed by Mr Sutton, bicycling very upright and using his toes, and two day boys went past at a moderate precincts riding pace. Then came Stanhope on foot, wondering whether to speak.

"Are you happy?" said Stanhope. "Can I do anything for you?"

"I'm all right," said Sandy. "I'm just working a chiz on Trevithic."

"It would be better if you didn't," said Stanhope. "But you will if you want to, won't you?"

"Well, yes," said Sandy. "But he was trying to be friendly yesterday."

"A friendly chiz is different," said Stanhope.

"Oh, this isn't friendly," said Sandy. "It's quite enemy-ish, as well as being secret, but I'll tell you if you like. I'd tell you anything."

"Don't tell me," said Stanhope. "I only chiz people if it's quite friendly, and it never is."

"I know," said Sandy; and he wondered whether to abandon the bonfire-stealing plan.

"You do want to be a chorister, don't you?" asked Stanhope. "I saw you looking up theory."

"It's all right looking," said Sandy. "But a lot of it's listening too, and I can't do it if I know before I start what I'm listening to."

"You do need help," said Stanhope. "My mother helped me in the evenings. She knows quite a lot about it now."

Sandy pointed out that he was a boarder, and, remembering how he had offended Paterson yesterday, did not boast to Stanhope of how he had refused Trevithic's help.

"I'll help you," said Stanhope. "Because you're Decani."

"You can help me if you want," said Sandy. "I like you."

"I like you sometimes," said Stanhope, and Sandy wanted to shout that out to the world; but instead he framed the thought and hung it up in his mind where he could always see it, and almost forgot it again when Stanhope said, looking thoughtfully with his big eyes at Sandy: "I like most people."

Sandy hated the thought for a moment, and then considered that it showed Stanhope's generosity, and that he hardly said it to everyone, or even to most people. "Michael," said Sandy, more or less in a question.

"Yes," said Stanhope. "If you like."

"But everyone calls me Sandy, even at home."

"Trevithic doesn't," said Stanhope. "Anyway, the others will see us in a moment. Let's go to the second form during break, and use the piano."

"Yes," said Sandy. "Thank you."

They parted, and Sandy went to school to sort out the things he had in mind. They were, that he would not on any account repulse Stanhope, because there was no one like him; and that to spite Trevithic (unless he became low and humble) he would not be a chorister, so Cantoris would have the chorister and that would be that.

But, and this was most important, Sandy thought he would know as much, perhaps, as Trevithic. And, of course, it all upheld Stanhope's idea of equality. Trevithic wanted all to be choristers: Stanhope wanted all to be singing boys who were as good as choristers.

The bell rang. Sandy ran in to wash the workshop grime from his hands.

CHAPTER 14

A Recipe Given

Paterson was studying the notice board when Sandy walked through the passage.

"What are you face-making about?" said Sandy.

"Ssh," said Paterson. "Mr Ardent's in the kitchen. He's just put this up." The warning was a good one: no talking in the passages was an old rule. Sandy looked at the new notice. It read:

"CHORISTER'S TEST, Saturday, 29th October.

From four o'clock in the practice room.
  i. Sight Reading, to simple accompaniment
 ii. Sight Reading, unaccompanied
iii. Sight Reading of second treble part
 iv. Plainsong
  v. Ear Tests
      4.00 Miller; 4.15 Collins; 4.30 Sandwell;
      4.45 Paterson; 5.00 Meedman; 5.15 Tribe

At 5.30 in Form 3.
 vi. Musical Theory Test
vii. History of Music test
viii. writing down of simple two-part tune heard
      three times only.

T. Sunderland."

"It looks nice," said Sandy. "I don't think I'll go."

"He can't want any choristers," said Paterson. "Not if he wants all those things as well."

"Go on," said Sandy. "You could do it, then the new chorister would be Cantoris: slight chiz for Decani."

Mr Ardent came out of the kitchen.

"No Mothers' Meetings in the passage, please," he said. "There is a rule, Sandwell, Paterson."

"Sir," they both said, and went away to the fourth form to sit down for further consideration of Dr Sunderland's notice.

"It's no good," said Paterson. "They'll never make me a chorister, because I can't write down simple tunes in two parts: I can't really do it in one part."

"Well," said Sandy, "I don't want to learn any more

about it. I'll help you."

"How?" said Paterson. "Wouldn't Trevithic?"

"No," said Sandy. "He's Decani."

"So are you," said Paterson.

"I'm not so Decani as Trevithic," said Sandy. "He's absolute dashing Decani, but I'm not." He felt that this idea would seem rather Philip-Sidney-ish – "Thy need is greater than mine" – if he abandoned his own chance and helped the pathetic enemy. The idea would seem right even to Trevithic, who would have to acknowledge it. For Stanhope to help Paterson direct seemed a bad idea, and Stanhope was Decani and probably not interested in Cantoris chances.

"Secret," said Sandy. "I'll help you by playing piano notes you can't see."

"And if we can listen to the different intervals," said Paterson. "If *I* play them, I forget them, because sometimes the same one looks different in different keys, although it sounds the same."

"We'll do it after dinner," said Sandy. "As soon as duty patrol's over: we needn't go to rest."

"All right," said Paterson. "Not enemies?"

"Never," said Sandy. "I swear in E flat not to be." That was a new oath, and it sounded very impressive. "You've got to swear it too, in the relative minor," said Sandy, and Paterson swore it in C minor. At break Stanhope took the *Exposition*, found the page of suggested ear tests, and played for Sandy the intervals, chords and arpeggios he found there. Then he made him sight-read in both piano clefs and in the alto clef, used for plainsong.

"You don't do too badly," said Stanhope. "We could do some more after evensong, couldn't we?"

"Yes, please," said Sandy, "and I'll see if I can get those things right like you playing D and making me sing A flat."

"Or A double-flat," said Stanhope, and they had to stop because of the end of break.

Sandy passed on his new information after dinner. "It would be funny if I were teaching you to be a Doctor of Music," he told Paterson. But he did not tell him where he got the substance of the lesson, nor did he tell Stanhope how his instruction was used. After supper he went on with Paterson again, using up Stanhope's after-evensong lesson.

At breakfast on Thursday came a long-expected announcement. Everyone had been waiting to hear that the bonfire and the Guy Fawkes could be made, and who was authorized to do it.

"We'll have to be careful," said Mr Ardent. "It's a privilege given to us by the Dean and Chapter: they very much dislike having large fires and fireworks in the precincts, but they know how we enjoy them, so they let us do it once a year. The rules are, that all fireworks are kept by me in the study. No fires are to be lit before the fifth, people must only go to number thirteen when a prefect is there, and no fireworks are to be ignited except by adults, Silverman."

"No, sir," said Silverman, who had a habit of spectacular experiment.

"And we cannot have hordes of people making nuisances of themselves at the Chapter workshop, looking for wood and sawdust. Only Trevithic or Madington can go in, but others may, of course, help to carry the sacks here. The prefects build the guy in their hut. When it's done, you'd better put it in the hall,

Trevithic."

"Choir school totem," said Madington.

"One more thing," said Mr Ardent. "No bicycle tyres on the bonfire. Last year we almost choked Canon Fredley, and he was *not* amused."

Sandy wondered what Trevithic would say when he found the shavings already captured. He built a conversation round Trevithic's humble requests to be allowed to share, and watched him and Madington go out immediately after breakfast to see the Pargales. Ten minutes later they came running back in competition, raced through the school, and went to the prefects' hut. They came out peaceably, and Sandy waited where he might meet them in order to bargain with them about the wood-shavings. But, though they saw him, they took no notice, and their announcement was that there would be a bonfire, but no guy.

"Why?" said Sandy, asking the question to the general air, so that somebody would take it up and ask Trevithic.

"Why?" said Trevithic, when the question came to him. "Somebody took the wood without permission, but it isn't anyone we bother about, so we shan't do anything about it." But he said nothing about the two sackfuls of something in the prefects' hut already.

Trevithic's attitude was so sensible that when Sandy found it angered him, it was anger against himself, not against Trevithic. The only way out of the anger was to offer Trevithic the shavings without bargaining, but it was easier to forget the matter. It was one thing to be an outlaw accidentally, and quite another to have to act like one all the time, breaking the law again and again, like or not like.

The solution was to make a guy himself, and present it to Trevithic without saying who it was from. He thought about the idea down the length of the passage, and it would have vanished away like most ideas as soon as he reached the yard, had he not heard Lowell, in the fifth form, saying: "It's one of Sandwell's wet schemes again. But Trevithic says we've not to do anything about it."

"He wants to make us look like fools, somehow," said Beale. "Sandwell does, I mean."

"Dim and spiteful and wet," said Lowell. "Hopeless."

Sandy avoided running into them by going up the spiral staircase. "Hopeless," he thought. "I'm not. And I'm not doing anything wet, only making the guy instead of Trevithic."

In that case the guy would have to be clothed: they are built from the outside inwards, first the raiment and then the man. He went up the staircase and along to the linen room, where there might be old clothes for disposal. When he got there he stayed out in the passage, because Trevithic and Madington were there first, and he did not wish to be seen. "Too big," Trevithic was saying. "We did have two sackfuls of shavings, but we tramped one into the floor, and now we've only got half each."

"They'll both be very small," said Madington. "Those old pyjamas are much too big."

"We can't make only one," said Trevithic, in answer to a question. "It would be too small. But we can make two little ones, because they could be quite small."

"Both very horrible," said Madington.

"Mine will be called gargoyle," said Trevithic. "It'll

be the oddest thing in the world."

"So will mine," said Madington. "Even odder. It'll be heathen for one thing, and all gargoyles are Christian."

Trevithic argued that gargoyles notably never went into church.

"All right," said Madington. "Mine's not merely a heathen; it's a heathen god. Baal, or somebody."

"As for the gods of the heathen, they are but idols," said Trevithic, singing a slidy piece from an anthem.

"Mine will be a sort of idol," said Madington. "An odd god. A goddity. The goddity."

"Gargoyles and goddities," said Trevithic. "I'd better go and ring the bell."

Sandy escaped into the empty day room to let Trevithic by, and Madington stayed for a moment in the linen room discussing with them in there how to make small goddities, and came out with an answer, but what it was Sandy did not know.

He followed Madington downstairs, wondering whether it was worth making a third guy, and whether it was safe to ask the linen room for old clothes: they would tell everyone about it, and who it was that asked. There might be, perhaps, another way of getting clothes.

He went to practice in his usual place in the line, the first time there for several days, where he could see in front of him Stanhope's head, and find beside him Paterson, his only two friends.

CHAPTER 15

Idols

Sandy lost most of his mid-morning lesson with Stanhope. Before they had been at it very long Trevithic came into the room, on his way out from cocoa-serving.

"You should be on the Oaks," he said. "You didn't come out yesterday, either."

"I'm afraid we're busy," said Stanhope in an entirely cool manner.

"I wanted to ask you something, as a matter of fact," said Trevithic.

"Me or him?" said Stanhope. Sandy thought he might have known what Trevithic would say.

"You, of course," said Trevithic, as if nobody would want anything from Sandy.

Stanhope defended Sandy by saying, "I told you we were busy", but a stronger defence he could not give. "And why should he," thought Sandy. "I'm not much good at the things Trevithic does."

"It's a private talk," said Trevithic.

"We're private now," said Stanhope. "And busy."

"You should be outside," said Trevithic. "That's a school rule. And you know what we decided about Sandwell."

"We've decided something else, now," said

Stanhope.

"All right," said Trevithic. "It's *your* time: you waste it."

"I will," said Stanhope. "Or at least, I shan't."

"Won't you?" said Trevithic. "I'm only warning you. Though he might be all right."

Sandy had had enough argument: he knew that Stanhope's time would be wasted, even though Paterson had the benefit of it in the end. The only satisfaction was that his acts were annoying Trevithic, who had wounded him with silence. Yet even that satisfaction seemed improper, because he felt that Trevithic was right. He left Stanhope and Trevithic together, and went out alone to the Oaks, and stayed there alone until the end of break, looking at the *Exposition* and learning it.

In the five minutes before dinner he ran round to number 13 and looked behind the angel into the tree trunk at the wood-shavings. They lay there in an idle white nest, at present quite useless without clothes to hold them. He put the angel back and left number 13 again, opening the gates with caution on his way out.

His lesson with Paterson after dinner was a difficult one, not so much because of the subject, but because Trevithic might have come in at any moment and sent them up to rest, and scolded Paterson for talking with Sandy. But there was no interruption, only the thought of it.

Stanhope helped again after evensong, and Sandy did the lesson again with Paterson before bedtime, and went to bed knowing that Trevithic looked on him with great severity.

In the morning, putting on his trousers, he had an

idea about the wood-shavings. After matins he put the idea into operation, and caught Dr Sunderland as he left the organ loft.

"'Mph?" said Dr Sunderland, when Sandy asked him the question he had in mind. "Have I wha'mph? I can't say; I'll look 'mph see. Come to 'mph house at eleven, and I'll do wharrumph can f'you."

"Thank you, sir," said Sandy, and went to go back to school through the cloisters, because the conversation had taken him along the nave a little way.

As soon as he opened the door to the cloisters he saw Trevithic, Madington, Beale, and DeMaris, in a bay of the cloisters, conferring together in secrecy. Trevithic and Madington were unwrapping two little paper bundles, and when they had undone them they held up for examination what was in them. Sandy held the door ajar and watched: he was too interested to be polite. They had solved the problem of dressing the two tiny guys, the gargoyle and the goddity.

"Good thing people have sisters," said Trevithic. "I didn't ever think dolls would be useful," and he held up a pair of woollen leggings with blue bobbles at the ankles.

"She requires ten pence for them," said DeMaris. "It should have been fifteen, but in view of the nature of the purpose for which they were intended, I bargained to ten."

"Linen-room stuff would have been free," said Madington.

"But no use," said Trevithic. "I've even got a hat with this lot."

"But no head," said Madington. "I've only got this thing." He waved a white thing like a night-gown eighteen inches long.

"And a sock," said Beale. "You must gather the hem into the top of the sock and sew it up, and then fill it from the top and put a head on."

"One-legged goddity," said Madington. "How much?"

"Seven pence," said Beale. "It was mine, really. I mean, I had to wear it when I was a baby. It's a bit like a surplice, isn't it?"

"Fancy an important heathen goddity wearing second-hand clothes," said Madington. "It's his skin as well, so he'll be a second-hand Baal."

Sandy wondered whether to walk past in a knowing way, or whether to turn round and go up through the Cathedral again. It was decided for him by Turle, who pulled him from the door and closed it firmly.

"We try to keep the building warm," he said.

"Sorry," said Sandy. "But I suddenly didn't want to go that way."

"You ought to be in school," said Turle, who could never approve of odd boys walking in his Cathedral.

Sandy went out by the usual door, and at the bottom of the steps came across the four prefects hurrying back and counting out money among themselves, after one of Madington's invented methods.

Sandy walked past without seeing them, purposely, and found Stanhope in school. He explained that at break he had an engagement with Dr Sunderland, but thought it better to say nothing of the reason for the engagement. Nor did he mention Trevithic's gargoyle clothes or Madington's goddity garment.

At break Dr Sunderland was in his house, next door but two to Turle, in the row by the precincts gateway.

"Have 'mph slice toast," he said. "Honey on 'mph."

"Thank you, sir," said Sandy. "Very good honey."

"Made 'mph myself," said Dr Sunderland. "I mean bees made 'mph." He kept hives of bees in his little backyard, with houses all round, and the bees had to fly all over the city for flowers. "Now, will one of these pairs do?"

He had brought down and laid on the piano two old pairs of trousers, one grey flannel with the seat polished thin by the organ stool, and the other brown corduroy with the velvet breaking away.

"Either would do," said Sandy. "The grey ones might be easiest."

"Good," said Dr Sunderland. "Size smaller than 'mph others: never get myself into 'mph again."

"You haven't got a jacket, have you, sir?" said Sandy; but Dr Sunderland shook his head. "It's trousers that wear out," he said. "Ask Turle. He's just gone across to his house."

Sandy thanked Dr Sunderland again, and went to Turle, who was, as usual at eleven o'clock, eating a scone and drinking tea.

"Clothes?" he said. "Jumble sale?"

"Guy Fawkes," said Sandy.

"'Images of the heathen'," said Turle. "'They that make them are like unto them'."

"Dr Sunderland said you might have a jacket," said Sandy. "He gave me some trousers."

"Show me 'em," said Turle. Sandy unrolled them and held them for Turle to inspect. "Too good to burn," said Turle. "And we're here and there of a size. I'll give you something really worn out."

He took the trousers, leaving Sandy standing on the

doorstep with the precincts pigeons bubbling and waddling round him, watching for Turle's scone crumbs, which he always threw out of the window. He came back in a few moments with a blue bundle that unrolled into a Turle-sized boiler suit, with brass buttons.

"There," he said. "Little holes burnt all over it from leaving it in the Chapter workshop and Pargale borrowing it. But it'll stuff up, if you've got enough stuffing."

"Plenty of stuffing," said Sandy. "Enough, I think."

"It won't take all that," said Turle. "I'm not fat. Tie up the legs and the sleeves, put a head on it, and there you are."

"I wonder who we shall name it after," said Sandy.

"Be off," said Turle, and closed the door.

Sandy went down to number 13. The gates were open, and eldest and middle Pargale were there, throwing away stones removed from the cloisters.

"You'll put the fire over here," said eldest Pargale, leaving middle Pargale to move the stones alone. He walked across the beech leaves and showed Sandy where the fire should be, not near the beech tree itself, spreading from the mound that had been a bell tower seven hundred years before, nor near the walls of the houses that backed on to the precincts.

"I'll tell Trevithic," said Sandy. "They won't build it until tomorrow afternoon, when I shan't be there."

"Nor shall we, Dad," said eldest Pargale.

"Not in winter, Dad," said middle Pargale, and youngest Pargale was not there to say anything.

Sandy uncovered the wood-shavings, sat on the cold stone angel, and began to fill Turle's boiler suit. He had to stop after two minutes, because the shavings came tumbling out of the arms and legs and neck. He went to middle Pargale to beg some string. Middle Pargale looked in his pockets and found nothing. He came and looked at the body of the guy to see what was wanted.

"He'll want a bellyful," he said, when he read the measurements on the label in the neck-band. Then he went to eldest Pargale, said "String, Dad," and felt in eldest Pargale's pockets until he found what he wanted. Eldest Pargale contemplated the ground all the time, working out how to arrange the stone they had to bring in. Middle Pargale tied up the arms and legs of the guy, and said: "It hasn't a head. We've one off a queen: ask Son for it."

"Now?" said Sandy. Middle Pargale said "Yes". Sandy ran across the precincts again to collect the head from a queen.

CHAPTER 16

Queen's Flit

Youngest Pargale was working at the back of the upper workshop. Sandy went up the stairs to him.

"You, Dad?" said youngest Pargale, going on with his chisel tapping.

"It's me," said Sandy. Youngest Pargale put down his mallet and chisel, blew away the last-sliced yellow coil of oak, rummaged in his memory, and said: "Peter Sandwell."

"Yes," said Sandy. "I've only got five minutes now, and they've sent me for the queen's head to put on a Guy Fawkes."

"Merry Antonet," said youngest Pargale, remembering his schooldays. "Not that it *is* Merry Antonet, but she lost her head on a gullet-knife."

"Like M.Q.S.," said Sandy, using Mr Lewis's abbreviation, "a Queen of Scots."

"Don't know who this one's queen of," said youngest Pargale. "But somewhere, for sure. She has a fixy look, like any queen. You'll see."

He led Sandy downstairs again, to where the head was kept, high up on an almost-outdoor shelf, looking up into the underwebs of the roof tiles.

"We tipped her, for her looks," said youngest

Pargale, and brought the head down, blowing the dust off. He turned it round, and it looked at Sandy.

"No crown," said Sandy. "She does stare at you, doesn't she?"

"Looks like lightning," said youngest Pargale. "Though she's been stove in at the back."

The head was life-size, and made of papier-mâché, thickly painted, and more thickly coated with dust. The back had been broken in, but the face was still queen, and looked at Sandy (if Pargale held it so) as if he were a slug in the cabbage.

"She ought to be blindfold," he said. "They do blindfold people when they burn them."

"Welcome to do it," said youngest Pargale, and found the end of a rag and tied it over the head's eyes. "She looks more bonny now," said Sandy. "Thank you very much."

He looked up at the Cathedral clock as he went by, and found it was a minute slower than the workshop clock, which was one of the useful kind that stamped the time and date on a paper if you pulled a lever. Sometimes the operation stopped the clock. Sandy had two or three minutes in hand, depending on which clock the school went by.

Middle and eldest Pargale were still at number 13, arranging their stones. Sandy showed them the bandaged head, and then put it and the boiler suit among the shavings in the tree trunk, and rolled the angel against the hole again.

"You keep her wrapped," said eldest Pargale.

"She'll watch you out, else, won't she, Dad?" said middle Pargale.

"She was worse before she had mice, Son," said

118

eldest Pargale, looking at the ground again. "She'll damp off in the tree, Dad. Bring it all back when it's done, and we'll put it in the clerk's office."

"I will, later," said Sandy. "But the bell's going and I'll be late."

He ran back to school, tailing in with the others, and went to the fourth form. Mr Lewis, when he came to take them, sent him out again to wash off the dust the queen's head had left on his hands.

"Have you been digging *drains*?" he said. "Or have you a secret *toffee*-mine, or have they been like that since *yesterday*?"

Sandy went to wash without answering: some of Mr Lewis's questions did not need answers. He washed in the changing-room, amongst the mixed smells of carbolic soap and football boots; and as he did so he realized that for two or three days he had not felt lonely, and that silence was rather peaceful. The reason for not noticing silence so much was that he had had something to do all the time: either the *Exposition* or the lessons that went with it. He dried his hands on the clean edges of the towel, and went back to the lesson.

The free spaces of the rest of the day went by quickly: all the faster because tomorrow brought the chorister's test. It was a thing that had to be done, but nothing would come of it. Though if they did make him a chorister, and everyone spoke to him again, would they all the time feel slightly superior because they had forced him to it? Would they feel just as superior if he failed? And, most of all, what would Stanhope say? Did he owe Stanhope's friendship to Stanhope's certainty that he would be a chorister?

With these thoughts all among the wood-shavings Sandy stuffed Turle's boiler suit during the afternoon. When it was full, it would stand up, if one hand supported its back. But it would by no means go again into the tree trunk, even when he crawled in himself and gathered up all the rest of the shavings left over. Sandy put last week's local newspaper over the neck hole, to keep the shavings in, and went to look for a piece of wood and a nail. He found both in a broken handcart, left there with a broken wheel by one Pargale or another. He worked a nail out, and banged it through the top part of the queen's head, into the piece of wood, and thrust the wood through the newspaper, at an article that read: "City Fathers Approve Estimate. Cllr. Grey in full agreement." Mr Ardent was a City Father, because he was on the council. Sandy jammed the head down without reading further to see what was approved of, and let the queen look about her. She obviously thought she was in a poor state, because the nail came out and the head fell off, but a little more hammer-work put her on again, staring critically over Sandy's shoulder.

"Well, I can't leave you here, ma'am," Sandy told her, inspired to politeness by her manner. The damp had already crept into the boiler suit, and was probably settling in the head as well. "She may sneeze," said Sandy. "I should die of fright."

There was another strong reason for moving the guy away: on Saturday afternoon the rest of the boarders would be building the bonfire here, and they would certainly explore the tree trunk. There was the Pargales' offer, and Sandy decided to break one more school rule in order to take the guy along there after dark, and then relax into an orderly life. "Probably as a chorister," he thought. "That would be something."

He left the guy on the grass, with the queen unblindfolded staring haughtily at the sky.

After supper, at the time when no one was allowed outside again, he went out, into darkness little more than twilight, because the moon lay over Canon Fredley's garden, having got up before dark. He took the guy up, tucked the head under his arm, and dragged the rest by the buttons, across the asphalt on to the grass, and walked quickly along the margin, with the two legs of the guy shuffling behind him, one on the green and one on the gravel. The workshop gates were closed, but the secret of opening them was more widely known than a secret should be: you trod on the bar of the left-hand gate, lifted the right-hand one, pulled outwards, and pushed inwards, and the gates were unlocked. Sandy put the guy in the sheltering overhang of the roof, beside the ticking time-clock, putting the head on backwards, to stare less, left the workshop, closed the gates by operating the opening secret in reverse and sprinted back to school, all against the shadows of the Cathedral buttresses, and no one saw him. He came in warm and breathless, trying to look innocent, and gave Paterson the last helping lesson the *Exposition*.

"I shall never be any good at it," said Paterson. "I have to count on my fingers."

"So do I," said Sandy, who had always been a little ashamed of the fact before. "So I'm as bad as anyone."

"It'll be somebody naturally brainy, not one of us at all," said Paterson. "I know it will."

"Won't be me," said Sandy. "But if it's you and they know I taught you, that's as good as, without being a win for Trevithic."

CHAPTER 17

The Cake in Sight

Sandy stood facing the Treasury clock, keeping well away in case he stopped the official Cathedral time by touching the pendulum with his shoulder.

The clock said "Ting" for half-past four, and footsteps sounded on the practice room stairs. Collins came down, and turned off the light as he came: last man always should.

"You next," he said.

"What's it like?" said Sandy.

"Not to say," said Collins. "Only, deadly."

"Oh," said Sandy. Now that the time was so near – a stair-climb away – he forgot whether he wanted to be a chorister, and thought that here was a test that must be passed or trouble would ensue.

He lengthened the stair climb by going up in the dark, guiding himself by the gleam of daylight through the door at the top. But the end came at last, and Dr Sunderland, with the test, waited in the daylight beyond the door.

"Sandwe'mph," said Dr Sunderland. "Take the top book, the service, and look at the first page of the Benedictus. I'll give you a few minutes to study 'mph, and then you can sing 'mph."

Sandy looked at the semi-quavered page, and read the composer's name: T.A. Walmisley. "1814–1856," said Sandy to himself, but the dates were of little use in the singing. He gazed at the page, without finding out anything from it, except that the closer he looked, the blacker it was. So he shook his head, put his finger under the key signature, and worked out all the details, according to the method of the *Exposition*, and found that the result agreed with what he had automatically thought when he saw the page: you get used to a method of seeing half and guessing the rest. He went through it bar by bar, working out beforehand where he would get lost and how he could start again after a silent bar: he knew that some quick leaps were beyond him, but by stopping before them and watching them go by on the piano he could restart on a chosen note, if Dr Sunderland did not go too fast.

"Ready'mph?" said Dr Sunderland.

"Yes," said Sandy, and put his finger below the beginning bar of symphony, picking up his starting note and keeping it in mind, until "Blessed be the Lord God of Israel". He started, found the melody, stayed with the accompaniment, skipped two fiddly pieces and caught up again (though it meant talking about "thy ant David" instead of "thy servant David"), and would have been ready to turn the page into uncharted territory, but Dr Sunderland stopped, without making any comment on the singing, and said:

"Bright Oriana next. First page, treble line, sixteen bars. Unaccompanied. Here's 'mph note G. Look at 'mph music first, same as last time."

Sandy looked at the music: a madrigal, written by "Anon", who was, of course, what they call anyone unknown.

"Ready?" said Dr Sunderland, after a very short time, Sandy thought.

Sandy said "No."

"Mph," said Dr Sunderland, meaning "wrong answer but have some more time, all the same."

He asked again very soon, and Sandy said "Yes."

Dr Sunderland gave him the note again, and Sandy sang to him how Bright Oriana, lately risen, had put Phoebus to shame, and would restore everlasting day. Oriana was Queen Elizabeth, he knew, but Phoebus was unknown, like "Anon".

"Call 'mph Feebus, not Poobus," said Dr Sunderland at the end. "Next the Stanford second-treble part."

Sandy went through the page of Stanford, sure that he would be caught here, with an upper part against him. But when he came to sing he found the piano less distracting than voices at the higher pitch, and at the end thought he had come through reasonably well.

Dr Sunderland gave no sign of pleasure or displeasure. "Plainsong Magnificat, fourth tone, third ending."

Dr Sunderland gave him the note. Sandy started by singing "This is the intonation of the fourth tone, and this is the mediation, and this is the ending," singing each part as he named it: any words can be sung to Plainsong.

He sang four verses of Magnificat, and then Dr Sunderland stopped him and began to ask him instead to name intervals, sing the middle note of three, a perfect fourth on this, a minor third on that, the dominant on such a note, or the mediant in such a key.

"Enough," said Dr Sunderland after a time – much longer a time than Sandy liked. "Send up 'mph next boy. Don't talk about 'mph tests.

Sandy went out, and down the steps with the light on, and found Paterson on lonely sentry-go in the sentry-box arches of the chapel arcade.

"What's it like?" said Paterson.

"Ghastly," said Sandy. "I know I squawked," but the quarter hour had so quickly gone, except the last five minutes, that he could not remember his feelings during the time.

"Death us do part," said Paterson.

"He lets you have more time if you want it," said Sandy, passing on the little helpful information that he had.

Paterson made a face, and pulled himself up the stairs by the rope that did duty for handrail.

Sandy went out of the Cathedral by the south-transept door straight across to number 13, and watched Mr Lewis at the bonfire-building operations.

The fire was in the right place, where Pargale had said it must be, though Sandy had forgotten to tell Trevithic about it: if he had not forgotten he would still have said nothing, for fear of what Trevithic might say. He went on a tour of investigation, to see what had happened to the tree trunk. It seemed to be untouched, until he rolled the angel away and found Arle inside, pretending to be a dog guarding a house (or perhaps a half-wild Martian robot guarding a rocket). The moonlight flit with the guy had been necessary.

Mr Lewis saw him walking about, and sent him back to school.

"I know it's *hard*," he said. "But you've all next week to grub about and add to the *fire*: it won't hurt you to be turned into a *chorister*."

"I should think it will, though," said Sandy, and went back to school again.

At half-past five Dr Sunderland came to the third-form room, and gave each of the six candidates a typed question paper and a sheet of music manuscript. He first gave them the thrice-heard two-voice tune, playing it so that it was very easy to hear and distinguish which part was which. When he had dealt with that, he collected the papers, and sat with them under his great hands until six o'clock, collected the theory and musical history papers, and let them go.

"Tortures," said Paterson. "Nobody could know all these things."

"Nothing to fuss over," said Meedman. "We shall all have to do it again some other day."

"We should have done more lessons, Pat," said Sandy.

"*You* should have," said Meedman, which gave Sandy a chance to bang his head against a locker in a friendly way.

"Wait a minute," said Meedman. "When does he tell us?"

"Next week sometime," said Paterson. "Not sure when. But quite sure what."

"Trevithic says you're in silence until you're a chorister," said Meedman. "So I can't fight at present," and to avoid temptation Meedman went away.

"It'll be you, said Paterson to Sandy.

"Or him," said Sandy.

"But not the rest," said Paterson. "Not any of them."

Trevithic came in from the prefects' hut, with his hands covered in paint of several colours, on his way to borrow Vim to get it off with. He asked how the test had gone.

"Tweedledum said some of you weren't so bad," he said. "I saw him in the hall. What was it like, Paterson?"

"If we get through," said Paterson, "he's going to make us Doctors of Music straight off. At least, I should think he ought to."

"What was yours like, Sandwell?" said Trevithic.

"I wasn't listening," said Sandy, offhand and rude. "We shall hear next week."

"Monday," said Trevithic. "Do you think you've got through?"

"I hope not," said Sandy, and walked away. Why should Trevithic measure his thoughts so? The supper bell rang, and Trevithic hurried off for Vim, and the bonfire makers came to borrow it and to soak cold hands in hot water, and sniff macaroni cheese in the passage.

After supper Trevithic went through the theory paper, and Madington gave his opinion of the musical history. Sandy waited close by, listening, but trying to look as if he were reading. If Trevithic's answers were the right ones, then the paper had been easy, because the answers were Sandy's own. Paterson seemed to think so too, and went to fight with Meedman over long distance records with models in the passage.

Sandy went upstairs to the day room, found only Kelsey there, and walked in without permission. Kelsey went out, and put out the light, and came in again secretly to startle Sandy, but was startled himself by Sandy behind the door. They had a nocturnal slow fist fight around the room, until Lowell came in, sent them both away, and put their names on the Prefects' List for fooling about and endangering an aeroplane wing in building on the table.

CHAPTER 18

First Catch Your Cake

Sunday was a glowing sunny day, reminding Sandy of "Bright Oriana". Before the 10.30 service he ran round to the Chapter workshop because after thinking of Oriana he thought of the queen's head. He opened the gate, when nobody watched, and looked for the guy. It had been moved, and was not to be seen outside. That was all to the good: no one else would see it either, and it would see no one else, which didn't matter but was an interesting thought. The afternoon was free, and his own entirely, because it was his turn to sing at the evening service with all the smallest boys, and that meant he was let off the 3.30. He spent the valuable time building up the bonfire with dead leaves and any dry twigs that could be found in the garden of number 13. Paterson helped when he was free, and Stanhope came in to talk about the test and the questions on his way home from service.

Sandy thought it was time to prepare Stanhope for bad news, but Stanhope would only say: "I felt the same, but if you do something else, you don't feel it."

"What did you do?" said Sandy.

"Darned all my socks," said Stanhope. "My mother's very good at showing me how."

"I've got this to do," said Sandy. "But I've still got abdies about it. What if he does make me it?"

"You'd share my cake," said Stanhope. "What else is there?"

"It'd be disgraceful," said Sandy, without explaining that his pride would be the only loser.

Stanhope rode away, and Sandy went on pyramiding the bonfire.

Trevithic and Madington had been out on a city playing-field with Lowell, flying an aeroplane. They came back without it, because it had flown out of the playing field and into the "county gaol and house of correction", the other side of the wall. They came back to ask Mr Lewis's advice, because he had managed to recover aeroplanes before.

Sandy heard the conversation, because he had gone in to eat his emergency supply of chocolate, locked secretly and securely in the inkwell-hole of his desk: he

131

put the two pieces there every Saturday evening, to nourish him on Sunday.

"This time, Madington, there's no *escape*," said Mr Lewis. "You're an accessory after the *fact*, which means *Guilty*. It's obvious that you're sending files and skeleton keys to the *prisoners*."

"You could do it with a radio-controlled plane," said Madington. "Or with a rope from a helicopter."

"Bright ideas won't save you from the prison *cell*," said Mr Lewis. "Bread and *water*, Madington. You'd better write to the *Governor*."

"Go on, sir," said Trevithic. "You ask him again. Remember what he said last time."

"That it would *be* the last time," said Mr Lewis. "He'll know you're doing it on *purpose*."

"The Lord looseth men out of prison," said Madington. "Didn't you read the psalms this morning, sir?"

Mr Lewis went back with them, and left a tip with the porter at the gate, to bring the aeroplane back if the governor approved. "We burn 'em," said the porter, but Trevithic knew better, and added his own contribution to the tip.

By the time they had come back and told everybody of the negotiation, it was after six, and Sandy had come in to wash his hands before going to service. Trevithic and Madington went upstairs to play cards with Mr Lewis. Sandy went to the vestry to chase up the singing probationers.

Monday morning found a new tightness in the air. Sandy in particular felt it. Not only was there a bright dry frost, but there was a doubtful result to be announced during the day.

There was not long to wait. Dr Sunderland came punctual to practice at twenty to nine, and before he sat down he pinned a notice on the frame of the blackboard, higher than his head, where no one could read it.

"Psalms," he said. "Hundred and forty four'mph. Thirty-first morning."

"I think we know them well enough already, sir," said Trevithic.

"We sang them yesterday, sir," said Madington. "They've been used."

"V'well," said Dr Sunderland. "No psalms. Got a few things t'say 'mphstead."

"Read out the notice, sir," said Trevithic.

"Chorister's test Sat'day'mph," said Dr Sunderland. "Detailed result, and Badge Boy."

"Decani, of course," said Trevithic.

"Chorister," said Dr Sunderland, announcing his subject. "Great pleasure in springing 'mph slight surprise."

"Me," thought Sandy. "Drat."

"Appoint chorister who didn't expect 'mph," Dr Sunderland went on. "Best marks, tried hardest, pulls 'mph weight, credit to 'mph choir – " he paused to breathe.

"Not really like me," thought Sandy. Nor was it.

"Paterson," said Dr Sunderland.

"Well done, ye," said Madington. "May I go back, sir, and make a sacrifice to my heathen god?"

"Shurrumph," said Dr Sunderland. "Finish what I'm saying. Paterson works v' hard: be Badge Boy before long."

If Sandy had known before what dishonour and

shame he would now feel, what weight of wasted help, what burden of idle hours, would now press on him, and what soft bog of slipped chances and rivers of disdained advice were underfoot – if he had known how sharply these things would become apparent, he would have abandoned before he began on it the proud walk of the last weeks that led him down to this failed moment against a blue desk in the practice room. No scorn from Trevithic, or from anyone else, could touch him now; his heart was full of the arrows of his own remorse. Even Stanhope's noticing of his distress and touching his elbow, which would have seemed a divine condescension a week ago, meant nothing; he had snapped the bonds of his duty to please himself, and there was nothing left to hold him.

"Gives 'mph equal pleasure 'mph do another unexpected thing," Dr Sunderland was saying, but to Sandy the words were buzz: why was understanding always too late? "Paterson must come before 'mph, but another one who's worked solid, when he wants, c'n share 'mph cake. Are you listening to 'mph, Sandwe'mph?"

"No, sir," said Sandy.

"No interest to 'mph," said Dr Sunderland, "made you chorister, Sandwe'mph."

"Can't have," said Sandy, while he let the information soak in. All the doubts of a moment ago digested themselves and vanished, flavour and all, and instead of the seven devils of his last state was the warm grace of a reprieve.

"I thought you would, Sandy," said Trevithic. "You don't need to cry."

"I like crying," said Sandy, finding he had indeed

boiled over with tears on to the psalter, so that the third word of the morning's second psalm was "magnify", itself magnified by a drop of warm water. Stanhope felt in his pocket and brought out a white clean folded handkerchief, which he put into Sandy's hand.

Sandy tried to tell Dr Sunderland that Stanhope had done it for him with extra work at the *Exposition*, but the lavender-scented handkerchief baffled his words and none was understood.

Dr Sunderland explained that the others could try again at the next test; and then told Beale, of Cantoris, that he was to wear the badge. The quiet Decani applause left Sandy time to recover himself and stand up again.

"Cantoris wins," said Madington.

"No competition," said Dr Sunderland.

"Oh, no, sir," said Madington. "It's my heathen idol that did it, I think. I promised it a good sacrifice if we won. Some of those old sheep from Decani, sir, perhaps."

"As a matter of fact, Cantoris, we congratulate you on being two to one," said Trevithic. "We know that Beale deserves it, and we know that Paterson sings like a..."

"Valley full of corn," said Madington, thinking of the ones that laugh and sing in the psalms.

"Although he's so small," said Trevithic.

"Thank you, Decani," said Madington. "We are glad that you have Sandy for a chorister."

Dr Sunderland stopped the exchange of compliments by playing "Nuts and May", because the conversation sounded like the game.

"Leave 'mph psalms," he said. "You know 'mph

chants, don't you?" He played the chants through: though the psalms were the same, the music was different. "Descant, Decani, last verse last psalm evensong."

"Sir," said Sandy, with a sudden idea for showing his energy. "May I sing the descant solo?"

"'Mph?" said Dr Sunderland. "Why not? Practice 'mph first. Psalm 150 everybody."

They sang it, and Sandy lifted his voice above the rest in the last verse, and felt that it was a kind of flying.

"It'll do," said Dr Sunderland. "Paterson do 'mph end of next month."

"New tradition, sir," said Madington.

"Don't talk," said Dr Sunderland. "Heathen or not. Give out 'mph service books. Nearly nine already'mph."

CHAPTER 19

The Queen Reclothed

"Well done, all three," said Mr Ardent, in the Treasury chapel before matins.

"Well done, I agree," said Sandy to himself, feeling a size larger all over. And the "Well done" covered more than the feeling of belonging to the Cathedral: it covered the feeling newly returned of belonging to the Choir School, because in the vestry Trevithic had let rules go and said, without naming names, that they might all talk, anyone to anyone. So they had all talked to Paterson and Sandy.

After matins Trevithic said that conkers would be allowed again, if people were tidy, and from half a dozen cassock pockets came strings or bags of conkers.

"Well," said Meedman, "mine were in my locker, and they were taken. So were yours, Sandy."

"I got them back," said Sandy. "You should have looked in the dustbins."

Sandy was able to be generous at break, after going upstairs for the conkers. He found he was the richest owner, and the more he gave away the more there would be to win back and add to the champion's score. You could have a score as great as the number of conkers owned by the school. Or would you have to subtract one to allow for a solo conker starting as 0: not 1 until it had fought?

"I hope," said Mr Sutton after break, when Sandy and Paterson seemed disinclined to work, "I hope that your newly achieved dignity will not divert your attention from Dr Benjamin Kennedy's paragraphs on the impersonal verb."

Sandy looked at the list in Kennedy's Primer, to see whether anything appropriate was written there.

"*Licet*, sir," he said.

"What kind of answer is that?" said Mr Sutton. "It is lawful!" He had given the proper translation.

But someone had been at work with a pin in Sandy's copy, and made the English read "It is awful". Mr Sutton made him correct it, and went on with the lesson.

Evensong brought Sandy's solo descant. Dr Sunderland accompanied the psalm quietly, though it was the most joyful in the book, and let Sandy's voice rise above the rest of the music, so that even Canon Fredley looked up from the Bible at the Lectern, almost in approval.

"You've a nice voice," said Trevithic afterwards. "What's your highest conker?"

"Hundred and thirteen," said Sandy. "Only fought once."

"Hundred and ninety-two," said Trevithic. "Fought four times."

"Do you challenge?" said Sandy. Trevithic did, and they fought it on the Oaks under the breezy trees, until Sandy ended with a 305-er severely cracked, which would have to wait for an opponent in the same state, or worse, before fighting again.

On Thursday evening Sandy was taken from the

perfecting of a Wriggling Snake at Mah-Jong by a summons to a haircut in the senior bathroom. He gave Meedman instructions for finishing the Wriggling Snake, and went up to Mr Ardent.

"Your top-knot does seem to have run to seed," Mr Ardent said, wrapping him up in an old surplice. He combed hair over Sandy's eyes, and reviewed the top of his skull.

"I wrote to your mother last Sunday," he went on. "I thought she might like to be here when you were made a chorister on Saturday."

"It's a bit of a long way, sir," said Sandy. "I think she'll say no."

"She did," said Mr Ardent, putting the cold clippers behind Sandy's left ear. "There won't be another chorister-making until next spring: would you like to wait until then, so that your mother might be able to come?"

"I'd rather be done on Saturday, sir," said Sandy. "Ow!"

"Sorry," said Mr Ardent, shaking the jamming fluff out of the tweaking clippers. "Whenever you like. One more won't make any difference to the Dean,"

He snipped away at the back of Sandy's head, in silence for a while, and then bringing a conversation round to Sandy again: haircuts often involved you in a serious talk about yourself.

"I heard from Trevithic that you had captured all the wood-shavings, and left the school without enough to build a guy."

"I didn't do it purposely," said Sandy, not in excuse but in explanation. "The Pargales showed me the shavings, so I took them to the tree trunk in number 13, and got some clothes and built a guy out of them. I couldn't tell anyone about it, because no one was speaking to me. I didn't want to tell *them*."

"Will you produce this guy on Saturday?" said Mr Ardent, snipping the long front hair and letting the clippings fall on to Sandy's nose and cheekbones.

"Ffh," said Sandy, blowing hair away. "It's in the Chapter Workshop now, and I haven't thought about it since Friday night."

"Bring it when you can," said Mr Ardent. "I must stuff it with screechers and squibs. The other two guys I haven't been allowed to see."

"Madington says they're awful," said Sandy. "I think he worships his."

"The sooner it's burnt the better, I should say," said Mr Ardent. "Sorry again."

"Hardly felt it," said Sandy, because the pull had been his own fault for moving his head.

"I gather life's been a little difficult recently," said Mr Ardent, while he thinned the crown of Sandy's head.

"Sometimes," said Sandy.

"That's the way of the world," said Mr Ardent. "We don't find the right method at the right time: we always do it wrong the first time, and it can make things very trying."

Sandy agreed at once, very pleased that Mr Ardent saw the point so exactly. When the haircut was finished, Sandy swept up the hair from the floor and put it in Mr Lewis's waste-paper basket, which always angered him. "I'm not a dealer in *wigs*," he would say. "Take it *away*."

Sandy went to the Chapter workshop on Friday morning, to see what the guy was doing. Eldest Pargale, looking at the ground, recognized his feet, and raised his eyes to Sandy's.

"Want the lady?" he said. "She about, Son?" he asked middle Pargale.

"Not by, yet, Dad," said middle Pargale from round the corner. "Is she, Son?"

Youngest Pargale came to the open door of the upper workshop. "Let her stay a while, Dad," he said, after nodding to Sandy.

"Why?" said Sandy.

"Fine waste," said middle Pargale. "Son's got them."

"They got some worse at home, Dad," said eldest Pargale.

Sandy could not understand the conversation, and said so. Eldest Pargale raised his head and looked at the door above, and said, "He's got them."

Sandy saw what it was: youngest Pargale was wearing Turle's boiler suit.

"The lady's got his," said middle Pargale, and led Sandy to the clerk's office, which was a tiny room built against the Bishop's garden wall. Inside it lay a heap of wood-shavings, a terrible pair of old trousers, a tweed jacket, and the queen's head, eyeing with cold anger a bundle of estimates.

"Son'll ascend her proper," said middle Pargale. "Come in the morning, can't he, Dad?"

"He can come this time tomorrow, Dad," said eldest Pargale, and Sandy had to leave it at that. But he was glad to go away and venture the 305-er conker against a junior one just as cracked and worth fifteen. He won easily, with no further damage to what was now a 320-er.

On Saturday morning he forgot the guy entirely,

because Stanhope took him at break to the Treasury, to meet his mother, who was sewing the edge of a cope with a very fine scarlet thread. Turle was out of the way drinking tea at his own house. Mrs Stanhope gave Sandy a thimbly hand to shake, and asked him who he was, and how he was, and the general run of other mothers' questions.

Stanhope explained how they would share the cake between three of them, distributing it to the Cathedral clergy, and the choir, and then have the fragments for themselves. "We needn't give any to the singing boys," he said. "But I think it would be a good idea if we did, to show them that they aren't different."

"You can have my piece that's left," said Sandy, but Mrs Stanhope said that there was plenty of cake at home, and she was certain that there was little enough at school. Sandy thought that was fair, but it spoilt his generosity, so he withdrew his offer for the time being. "They don't usually have a cake on the same day they're made," he said. "I don't mean not new cakes, but not having cake as soon as you're a chorister."

Turle came back soon: he always did if anyone was sewing in the Treasury. He tried to send Sandy and Stanhope away, but they felt it was beyond his duty to send a son away from his parent. All the same, they gave in under Turle's strong eye, and went before the bell rang.

For evensong Sandy, Paterson and Beale lined up with the choir in the usual way, although they would not walk in with them at the beginning of service. "Wait at the north door of the choir during the first lesson," said Trevithic. "We'll come for you then."

"Butterflies in the tummy," said Paterson. "Caterpillars in the dinner: fainted ladies."

The remark reminded Sandy of the guy, which he had forgotten, and which was still in the clerk's office at the Chapter workshop. He wondered if he had time to race down and get it before the first lesson, but thought the risk too great. He and Paterson, when the rest of the choir had gone, leaned against the Treasury wall playing "Stone, Scissors, Paper" with their fingers, with Beale watching to see they made no noise. He stopped them when Sandy's raps on Paterson's wrist grew too loud.

They went down the aisle during the psalms, and stayed by Prior Tollelege's tomb while Canon Fredley read the first lesson, all about the taste of egg-white, and water blackish with ice, and the army of Sheba, which reminded Sandy of the queen's head again.

When Canon Fredley stopped, instead of coming out from the lectern, he waited, while Trevithic, Madington, and Mr Ardent came along the length of the choir, and arranged Sandy, Beale and Paterson in a line with linked hands, as if they had been playing "Chains" all over the Cathedral. With Mr Ardent leading, and Madington and Trevithic at either end of the line, they walked five abreast down the choir, until they stood in front of the Dean's stall, and the Dean looked down at them and cleared his throat.

CHAPTER 20

The Cake Consumed

"Mr Dean, I present to you Andrew Thomas Paterson, and Peter Sandwell, to be admitted choristers of this Cathedral; and Ivor John Beale, to be awarded a badge."

The Dean put on his spectacles, opened the door of his stall and stepped down. Mr Ardent pushed Paterson towards him, so that he took the right boy. The Dean led him by the hand to the end of Cantoris choir stalls, said "Kneel down," in a decanal whisper audible over the whole Cathedral, put his hand on Paterson's head and said: "Hehemn. Andrew Thomas Paterson, by the authority committed to me, I install you a chorister of this Cathedral Church. May the Lord grant you the will to obey, the power to lead, and the grace to accomplish the varied tasks of your position. The Lord watch over your going out and your coming in from this time forth for evermore. Amen."

Then, leaving Paterson, he came across to Sandy, took him to the end of Decani choir stall, and made him a chorister with the same blessing. Then he turned to Beale, who was brought forward by Trevithic. Mr Ardent handed him the badge, the silver and blue shield on an imperial ribbon. The Dean first tried to give it to Trevithic, who had a badge already, but Beale stepped forward to have it put over his head.

"Ivor John Beale," said the Dean. "Hehemn. I am pleased to give you this badge as a sign of appreciation for the services you have rendered this Cathedral by your work in its choir. Wear it as a sign of your authority in the choir, and honour the foundation that gives it to you, and may the Lord bless your work and service. Amen."

When he had finished, he walked back to his stall. Sandy stood up and stretched his ankle, which he had knelt down on crooked. Beale, Madington and Trevithic bowed to the Dean and went back to their places in their respective sides. Dr Sunderland looked over from the organ loft, and started the Magnificat with his hands and feet.

Sandy started his time as a chorister by missing the first lead altogether: he had accidentally picked up the anthem instead of the service.

Afterwards, when the choir had left the Treasury

and walked back to the vestry. Dr Sunderland played the music he had composed but not written down yet, called "Chorister's Cake Walk" which he always played as an outgoing voluntary when anyone had been made chorister.

"We shall have to alter the book-boys," said Trevithic. "You'll be Anthems, Sandy."

"Good," said Sandy. "Not today, though, is it?"

"No," said Trevithic. "I've only thought of it so far."

"Can I go?" said Sandy. "There's an important thing to do."

"There's the cake to have next," said Stanhope.

"I'll be back straight away," said Sandy, and Trevithic let him go.

Sandy ran through the cloisters towards the Chapter Workshop. Now was the time to get the guy: tea was early tonight, to allow time before bed for the juniors to enjoy fireworks; and before tea was the ceremony of the cake: it was not like a birthday cake, and could not be cut at a meal.

At the south-west corner of the cloisters he ran straight into Mr Sutton, who was walking today: he sometimes did walk if he was in no hurry.

"A bicyclist rings his bell before plunging at high speed round a corner," said Mr Sutton. "Have you a valid reason for this untoward velocity?"

"I was looking for a guy, sir," said Sandy.

"For a man?" asked Mr Sutton, suspecting Sandy of talking American.

"A Guy Fawkes," said Sandy. "To burn on the bonfire."

"I hope that your finding me does not imply the conclusion of your quest," said Mr Sutton.

146

Sandy remembered that at Mr Sutton's last school the boys had treated him cruelly, and might even have put him on a bonfire once, without having burnt him too much. "He's in the Chapter workshop," said Sandy.

"I trust you have the key," said Mr Sutton, and walked on.

"Shan't need the key," said Sandy to himself, and ran to the workshop. But he was wrong. It was Saturday afternoon, and the Pargales had gone home. Sandy opened the gates by the secret method and went in. The guy was nowhere out of doors. He looked through the window of the clerk's office, and there gazed the queen's head, on a stout well-lashed guy made from cast-off Pargale clothes. But the office door was locked.

Sandy left the workshop yard, closed the gates, and ran back to school, to fetch help of some kind. But no help was to be got at the moment, because Trevithic had set out from school to bring him back, and they met in the Dark Entry. Trevithic ran him along breathless to the dining-room.

The Dean was there, ready to cut the cake. Mrs Stanhope was next to him, with Mrs Paterson. The cake stood on a white table-cloth. It was a foot across, and iced in blue and white, with the Cathedral badge in the centre.

The singing boys cheered Sandy when he came in, and the choristers hustled him up to stand next but two to the Dean, beside Paterson who was beside Stanhope.

The Dean tried to stab the cake with a gentle stroke, but he only succeeded in scribing a mark across the icing, and making the knife bend like a bow.

"It's an old cake, sir," said Stanhope. "Would you like a shorter knife?"

"We may break the knives and leave the cake intact," said the Dean. "I remember breaking frozen plum cake with a hatchet beside the upper reaches of the Yangtse Kiang in China."

Owen had run for a knife, and with it the Dean daggered a sudden opening in the cake, and sawed out the first slice, which Stanhope put on a plate and gave back to him.

"Thank you very much, all three," said the Dean, and returned to eat the cake, while Mr Ardent came to cut the rest up: he was an expert cake-cutter. He sliced it neatly all round, and the three choristers, having laid aside what was due to the Canons of the Chapter, fed the two parents, left them talking to the Dean, and distributed slices to the choristers, the singing boys, and the boarder probationers, who were not really entitled to it.

In half an hour the cake melted away to a little brown triangular cliff with a patchy blue and white top.

"Shall we let Michael have the rest?" said Sandy to Paterson.

"Michael?" said Paterson. "Oh, Stanhope. Why?"

Sandy explained the way in which Stanhope had helped Paterson, by way of the lessons from the *Exposition*.

"Keep yourself a piece to send home," said Paterson. Sandy did that, and then insisted on sending the rest home with Mrs Stanhope, who invited him to come and finish it the next day for tea. He arranged it with Mr Ardent, saw Mrs Stanhope and Michael off, and then went to find Mr Lewis and see what could be done about the guy.

"Sandy, you would muddle it up," said Mr Lewis. "I

think one of the Cathedral keys will fit, but why you should bring me to housebreaking, I don't *know*."

They re-entered the workshop yard without using the key on the gate, and Mr Lewis found that the ordinary precincts key fitted the little office. He grumbled all the time about it, opened the door, and went in.

There was no guy.

"It must be here," said Sandy. "I saw it through the window."

"It can't be *hidden*," said Mr Lewis. "What's all this dust on the *floor*?"

"Stuffing," said Sandy. "Or exactly the same, anyway."

"You must have made a *mistake*," said Mr Lewis. "Or we shall solve the mystery in a *moment*."

Sandy could imagine no solution, but there was one, and they found it as soon as they came back to school and found the guy in the hall, keeping an eye on the study door.

"A Pargale brought it round," said Mr Ardent. "Did you forget it, Sandwell?"

"Well, sir, when I went they'd taken it to pieces and they were wearing its clothes: those are some old ones of theirs."

"These are rather good leather *buttons*," said Mr Lewis, examining the guy. "I should hate to see them *burnt*." He brought some pins from the study, pinned up the jacket where the buttons held it, and cut the buttons off.

"Vulture," he said, and took his prize away.

"Vulture's right," said Sandy. "It started with Dr Sunderland's bee-keeping trousers, and Turle exchanged them for a boiler suit, and then the Pargales took that, and now he's taken the buttons."

"Everyone seems to be one up on him, or her," said Mr Ardent. "She *has* a hard stare, hasn't she?"

"Wow," said Trevithic from the landing. He had met Mr Lewis and come to examine the guy. "It's a Gorgon, sir, turning people to stone."

"A gargoyle manufacturer," said Madington. "You make a face, let it look at you, and there's a gargoyle."

"It hasn't any fireworks in it yet," said Mr Ardent. "I'd better load it before supper."

"And I'll get my gargoyle," said Trevithic. "We'll have a trio of guys."

"That one soprano," said Madington. "Yours tenor, and my goddity terribly deep and bass."

They went to the prefects' hut to get them, and Sandy stayed to watch Mr Ardent load the queen's head with screechers and the arms and legs with bangers.

CHAPTER 21

The Last of the Idols

Trevithic had used a flour bag for a head and body, and the leggings for legs. His gargoyle had no arms, but it had a black face going all the way round the head, with three eyes, three noses, and three mouths, so that however you looked at it, it had a hideous twisted appearance. He had slung it on a pole, where it swung and dived and would not keep still.

"It's still frightened of the goddity," said Trevithic. "It menaces it in the dark."

"They'll be together in adversity soon," said Madington, bringing in the goddity covered in a sack. "I don't think they ought to see this thing in daylight."

Mr Sutton, on his way home, came through the hall and looked with an unfavourable eye on Trevithic's gargoyle. Since Mr Ardent was there, helping with another nonsensical guy, he said nothing about fireworks in general. He looked at Sandy's guy and said, "There is one among us whose buttons have been frayed off by the vicissitudes of experience. *Miseret*, Sandwell: it moves to pity."

"*Licet*, sir," said Sandy. "It is awful."

"*Vesperacit*," said Mr Sutton. "It grows late. I shall be home before the bombardment starts and we begin the ordeal by fire. What have you there, Madington?"

"Baal's grandson," said Madington. "Genuine heathen god, sir. But you no likee?"

"He has been helping you with your daily preparation, I surmise," said Mr Sutton. "You should engage the services of an educated idol, Madington. I believe there are several quite cultured gods in some of the eastern demonologies. As to that one, may I assume its immediate incineration?"

"We shall burn it as a heretic," said Mr Ardent.

"But you'd better not look at it," said Madington.

"The still gaze of the two visible deities is enough," said Mr Sutton, doing up his raincoat collar. "Their names are not, it is to be hoped, Shadrach, Meshach, and Abed-nego?"

He named the three men who had walked unharmed before King Darius in a fiery furnace. "You could prove they were burnt if you came and watched," said Trevithic, hoping to lure Mr Sutton to the bonfire.

"All the latest devices," said Madington. "Radio-controlled rocket range."

"Aimed at Canon Fredley's greenhouse," said Trevithic.

"Explosion pits," said Madington. "And a Big Bertha for blowing up bottlefuls of bangers."

"Special ramp for warhead screechers," said Trevithic. "Designed to go off at four-bar intervals."

"Pins all ready for catherine wheels," said Madington. "And seven-branched Roman-candlesticks."

"It's an extra-special display," said Trevithic. "Dr Sunderland is coming."

"You cannot induce me to abandon the comforts of my own fireside," said Mr Sutton. Sandy, who had seen the fireside, wondered how anyone could be comfortable at it. The floor was soft, with three carpets on it, but the chairs were hard upright ones, and the fire was a knobbly gas one that spluttered.

"We'll let you off, sir," said Trevithic. "Considering that you gave us a donation towards the display."

"Thank you," said Mr Sutton. "'Gift' is a better word, Trevithic: not every word of Latin ancestry is justified. Good night."

He took up his hat and went out into the dewed and mist-fallen dusk.

When he had gone, and the doors had closed on him, Madington uncovered the goddity.

He had, as Beale's sister instructed, gathered the skirt into the doll's sock, so that the body tapered to its ankle, and there was a perfectly good foot below it. The head had been constructed from balsa wood and fabric: the square edges and facets could be seen under the creature's hair, which was human hair rescued from haircuts in the senior bathroom (and from Mr Lewis's waste-paper basket), gummed on and gently brushed smooth.

The features had been carved in plasticine, after the style of the Aztecs in the *Geographical Magazine*. The face was very human in colour, and the eyes, looking narrowly at you, seemed to be determining the value of your sacrifice. Until this afternoon the arms had been of wood, but in the town after dinner Madington had visited a poulterer, and the arms were now two chicken's legs, with long strings knotted to the tendons, so that when Madington dandled the thing on his knee, sitting on the stairs, he could open and close the claws by pulling the strings.

Both the goddity and the gargoyle were painted in the brightest aeroplane colours in the school.

"It looks like some incredibly wizened and deformed mermaid," said Mr Ardent.

The bell rang for supper, and the two monsters were hung from the landing banisters, and turned the hall into an alchemist's den decorated with weird creatures. Mr Lewis said at supper that, coming that way, he had to turn back and walk downstairs by the spiral staircase.

Immediately after supper Mr Lewis went with all the probationers and singing boys, the camp lanterns and a gallon of paraffin, to light the fire. The choristers, old and new, stayed to wire on to metal rods inflammable heads of firelighter (the papery kind), and with one apiece they lined up in procession, while Trevithic and Madington balanced the Pargale guy on the Dean and Chapter handcart, and raised the goddity and the gargoyle on their poles high in the air. Mr Ardent subscribed a match, the torches were bunched and lit, spread again into the two by two procession, and moved off in the misty darkness round the end of the Cathedral. The red flames licked the air, and sparked on the overhanging ilex trees. The Pargale guy swung in her litter, and the two monsters swam their way through the air. The torches flared higher and higher, lighting the Cathedral walls all the way from apse to transept, and carmined the great central tower. The pigeons woke and complained.

The procession went gradually round to meet the answering yellow blaze at number 13. The fire blew strongly, and all the crowd of day boys, parents, and visitors came to the gate to meet the guys.

Dr Sunderland was there to see his trousers burn, but he did not know how they had been transmuted. Turle was there to see his boiler suit go; and he could not tell in the light of the varying flames what the guy wore instead.

Madington hung the goddity in the light of the fire and opened and closed its claws. Then, when the Pargale guy had been run up to the fire quickly and thrown on upright, the gargoyle and the goddity were hung on either side to catch the flames as they rose. The Dean and Chapter handcart was moved away at once "in case he burneth the chariots in the fire", said Trevithic.

The gargoyle and the goddity caught in a few moments: the claws twisted, the heads shredded away, and from their bodies burst screeching demons buried there, flung out to jerk and explode in the crowd.

In the middle of the fire the grim-faced queen, with

her fingertips smacking sharp thunderbolts, stared at the Cathedral; and as she stood there and fretted into ash, the flames curved her mouth into a smile, and as she smiled she tumbled down and turned to flame.